A KISS FROM A WOLFMAN

KISS FROM A MONSTER SERIES
BOOK 6

CHARLOTTE SWAN

For those of you who like to get a little knot-y...

For a full list of content and trigger warnings please go to the author's website.

www.authorcharlotteswan.com

PROLOGUE
CARYSSA

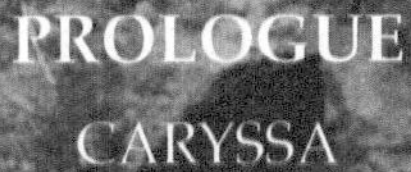

For the last sixteen years, I've been a captive in my own home.

If ever there was a chance to escape my royal prison, now would be the time. It's been over a month since I aided my brother's would-be bride, Laurelle, in escaping my family. It's the least I could do after I watched countless girls come and go, never to be seen again—all falling victim to my brother's cruelty.

Cruelty that he's inherited from our father.

Their shared temper had been on full display once I returned to the palace, bringing news of Laurelle's escape. Carysen, my brother, had been drunk. His rage had turned his face a few shades lighter than a plum. After his and my father's initial inquisition, I avoided him at all costs. Once they had been satisfied with my assessment that Laurelle had indeed overpowered me to flee, I was sequestered in my room with a host of guards stationed outside my door at all times.

Though they may have believed my tale, they still weren't entirely convinced of my innocence.

That is why I've spent the past month toiling away inside

these stone walls. My mother comes to me every so often—the only visitor I'm allowed beyond my ladies' maids. She tells me my father is growing more irate by the day. My brother has been dispatched to bring Laurelle to us, and I pray she has made it far beyond his reach.

She lives; I believe it in my soul. Yet that same sense of hope alludes me as I think about my future. My mother has become tense on her visits. I take her in now at the edge of my bed. An aging queen—her wrinkled face is pinched, and her blue eyes are too large.

As the guards resume their position outside the door, I make my familiar plea, knowing there is very little she can do to help me.

"Mama," I say softly, not to startle her as she stares out my third-floor window. "Can you please ask Father to release me from this room? I am growing restless. It has been a month, surely—"

"Your brother is dead."

My mother says it casually as if she is announcing that it may rain later today. My heart stumbles in my chest, and the needlepoint in my hand clatters to the floor.

"What?" The word is barely above a whisper. "Has someone sent word?"

Her face turns, and our matching eyes meet, yet they spark without recognition. Life inside this palace has made her a prisoner as well. The steel bars of her mind keep her contained— the woman she once was has long since perished behind them.

"Your father believes all of this is your fault."

Bile races up my throat.

"I—"

"You will be married—within the month. If you refuse to comply, you will be sent to the dungeon to live out your days with the rats." Her lids lower as her bony hand cups my cheek. "If I were you, I'd pick the vermin."

With one last pat on my cheek, she rises in a swirl of glittering skirts. Knocking once on the heavy wooden door, it opens and exposes the guards stationed outside. Like a ghost, she slips between the small opening and is gone—as if she had never been here. As if she was merely an omen of my forthcoming demise.

My hands begin to tremble as I play back her words. Moisture burns my eyes. Has my life been reduced to this—two miserable choices being forced upon me? I won't do it.

I think of Laurelle—of her curly hair and easy smile. When presented with the opportunity to flee and seize a future of her own choosing, she did not hesitate. Wherever she is now is better than any life she would've led shackled to my heinous brother. If I am going to survive, I will need to be brave like her.

The future I want is mine for the taking, and I will not pass up an opportunity to claim it.

Yet, the longer I stay in this room, the more I can feel my chances of escape sifting through my hand like grains of sand. Rising on stiff legs, I make the short journey to my door and try the brass handle. Giving it a tug, I'm met with familiar resistance as the lock holds fast.

A sigh slips from my lips, and I release the handle as if it has burned me. Even if the door had been unlocked after my mother's departure, the guards would ensure I didn't make it far. A dull ache pounds at my temples—my frustration slamming its fists against my skull.

Tears burn in my eyes, but I refuse to let any glide down my cheeks. I will be strong. I will escape. I will not let them steal my life and shackle me to some cruel man.

Even if it will take a miracle for me to get out of here.

Dark gold hair blows into my eyes from my loosened braid. I tuck it behind my ear and glance out the window, wondering if it has let in a draft. This room has been stifling my entire time in confinement. Another soft breeze tickles my cheeks, coming from the direction of my solid stone wall. I lower my brows as I take a tentative step closer.

It's not long before the wind picks up, causing the pieces of parchment on my desk to crinkle and thrash from the invisible force. The sweet smell of blooming flowers perfumes the air. This is all rather curious. I should be alarmed, but I feel a strange sense of calm and a bit of...hope.

Perhaps I have truly gone mad in this room.

I remain still as the fragrant breeze disturbs the inside of my room with its quiet intensity. The wind whips around me, blowing my hair and tugging at my clothes. A force more significant than my understanding is at play, and I am powerless to do anything but bear witness to it and hope it's here to aid me.

With wide eyes, I watch the heavy wooden door to my room swing open on silent hinges. A fresh breeze from the hall rushes in. I wait for the guards to storm in and demand to know what I've done—to punish me and remand me to the dungeon below.

Yet, as I wait to hear their clanking footsteps, none come. It is utterly still beyond my opened door. A gasp slips from my lips as I watch another improbable feat occur: the old dark cloak I have hanging from a peg in my room floats towards me. It lands gently on my shoulders. Invisible hands give me a reassuring, almost affectionate squeeze.

My mind immediately goes back to Laurelle. Could she have a hand in whatever is unfolding in front of me? Or have I succumbed to my despair in this room and am now hallucinating this whole thing?

Despite my confusion, I still tie the clock around my shoulders.

Without hesitation, invisible hands carry an old satchel I had resting against the wall towards me. The doors to my wardrobe peel apart, and various clothing items are carefully stuffed inside until the old leather is stretched to bursting.

All I can do is watch—the urge to scream and cower never comes.

The bag flies towards me, and the long strap loops over my head and drapes itself across my body. The weight is comforting and brings me back into my body. This is real and happening.

Finally, a coin purse made of sturdy brown fabric floats towards me. It hovers in midair. Glowing golden orbs swirl around the bag before solidifying into pristine golden coins. My jaw unhinges as I watch the coins fill the bag until it sags under their weight. There must be at least a hundred in there.

It glides toward me, and I manage to raise my hand. The heavy pouch settles against my palm—the weight a delight. This will be more than enough for what I have planned. Quickly, I tuck the bag away, not daring to question this wondrous gift.

Lifting my eyes, I survey my room one last time. I won't miss it, nor my life here, but I want to commit it to memory. My eyes lock on an open space in my room—nothing is there, yet I swear I can see something. A faint shimmering—a pulsing of air that makes me feel like whoever is responsible for this assistance is watching—waiting for me to claim this gift they've given me.

Squaring my shoulders, I inhale sharply.

"Whoever you are—whatever you are...thank you."

A gentle breeze blows over my cheeks in acknowledgment. The floral-scented air invades my lungs and strengthens my resolve once more. I don't have much time. Without a second look, I turn and quietly exit the room.

The hallway is eerily quiet, spurring me to walk faster. I move through the palace with a singular focus. I can taste my freedom—it coats my tongue like honey. The stone walls around me blur as I sail down flights of stairs and back corridors, careful to avoid lingering servants on their rounds.

I travel deeper and deeper into the bowels of the castle. With an arm wrapped around my leather bag, I'm careful not to let the gold coins jingle and give away my location. While I may be a princess, I've never had money of my own. My father and brother keep their coffers firmly locked. This money will buy me the future I've longed for.

Taking a sharp left, then another one, I rely solely on memory to navigate this labyrinth. I am far enough down that I should just have to pass by the kitchen, and then I'll be able to cross into the courtyard.

Pushing through another set of doors, I can smell the fresh scent of grass and—

Someone rounds the corner. A girl. She's young, draped in the white smock most of our scullery maids wear. Her face is gaunt, and a strand of reddish brown hair clings to her brow from underneath her handkerchief. My heart drops as she looks up, a sharp breath parting her pale lips.

If she makes a noise or alerts the guards in any way, I will be found out. Icy fear licks up my neck as I consider the punishment I will receive if I am discovered.

This young girl holds my whole future in her callused hands.

She pauses a few paces from me, bobbing into a half-hearted curtsey. When she rises, she takes me in from head to toe, from my fraying cloak to the bag strapped across my chest. Her eyes widen, and her dark brows lower.

"Please." It's the only word I can muster.

My heart pounds in my ears. Seconds pass, but they feel like years. Each shallow breath she takes causes my stomach to sink further. She twists her small hands into the front of the dress. Quickly, she glances over her shoulder before looking back at me.

"Through there leads to the garden." She uses a slim finger to point to a wooden door nearly concealed by the crumbling stone wall. "Go now. The cook is only a few paces behind me."

Gratitude floods me as I quickly reach into my satchel. If this girl is discovered to have aided my escape, she will suffer a fate worse than death. It is dangerous to linger here, but I must reward her kindness.

"Here," I say, dropping five gold coins into the front of her smock. "Leave here as soon as you can. Use these for safe passage."

Her eyes widened once more.

"Thank you," I whisper. She nods, her eyes shining.

Without risking exposing either of us more than I already have, I turn from her and yank open the hidden door just as footsteps approach from the end of the hall.

Once outside, the setting sun momentarily blurs my vision. The sweet, earthy scents of the garden swell around me. The damp grass soaks my silk slippers as I trudge through the greenery.

Quickly glancing around to make sure I am alone, I hurry through the tall hedges and underneath the swaying willows. The sound of sea birds calling overhead encourages me. It's not far now—I should still be able to make it.

As I pass underneath the final tree, leaves brush my cheeks and hair. The sight before me is glorious. Vast blue water as far as the eye can see. The orange sun is dipping below the horizon as pink tendrils coil in the darkening sky.

Glancing up, I stare at the top of the watchtower, only to find the loan guard on patrol asleep with his helmet off under the waning sun. Luck favors me once more as I travel down the sandy beach.

The wet sand makes it hard to keep my footing, but I manage it. The last rays of sunlight slip away as I reach the small dock. It is weather-worn, crumbling from time and seawater. Gruff voices of men can be heard as I approach.

Heavy dragging sounds echo down the dock as various objects are hauled aboard the vessel.

It is a large ship with blinding white sails and a polished deck. A couple nods to a man standing before a ledger before slipping aboard. I make my way over to him. The worn wood of the dock presses against my feet where my slippers have split.

The man before the ledger is older—with a graying beard and a deeply wrinkled face. His red captain's coat has seen better days as I take in its faded sleeves and worn buttons. He doesn't look up as I approach.

Clearing my throat, I wait for his eyes to meet mine.

"I'd like to buy passage on this ship. The further it can take me from here, the better."

The old man scoffs before slamming the ledger closed.

"We're all out of rooms." His eyes trail down my body, taking in the sorry state of my clothes and hair. "Besides, you couldn't afford it anyway."

With trembling hands, I reach into my bag and riffle around before producing what I need. I drop the ten gold coins atop his closed ledger.

"I'll take a private suite," I say, with more command than I've ever heard in my voice.

The old man raises his graying brows but says nothing as he sweeps my coins into his coat pocket. He opens his ledger and dips his pen into a small ink pot.

"Very well," he says. "Name?"

"What?"

"A name," he says, letting out a deep sigh. "Your name—doesn't need to be your real one. I just need something to put in the manifest."

Why did I not consider this before? I can leave no trail of my former self lest my family try and locate me. I wait for sadness to hit me, but it doesn't.

Instead, I feel unbridled joy at being able to shed this shackle of my past.

Princess Caryssa is no more—she died in that old room in the castle. I look up towards the darkening sky, and the first stars appear. They twinkle down at me in encouragement.

I think back to my first meeting with Laurelle—that innocent question she posed me in the carriage—now means much more.

A smile pulls at my lips.

"Stella," I say. "My name is Stella."

It is a name of my choosing—one that I will use happily to craft my future. Stella has no past—she is no one—a blank slate. My destiny belongs to me.

"Welcome aboard, Stella," the captain says. "Cabin three will be yours for the duration of our journey. We sail pretty far north—our final stop will be about two months from now."

I nod and walk towards the deck of the ship. It bobs before me, teasing me with its promise. A ship hand waits on the other side—a young boy with a round face and pale blonde hair.

"Miss?" he asks, extending a sunkissed hand towards me.

I take it and my first step towards freedom without hesitation.

1

STELLA

TEN YEARS LATER

Working nights at the Wolf's Fang isn't too bad. The patrons—humble farmers looking to spend their coins on a few mugs of ale after a long day—usually behave themselves. Not to mention, a single woman has very few job prospects in a village as small as this one.

Working at the tavern suits me, and the pay is decent. I've settled into a comfortable routine since landing in this farming town over five years ago.

It took me a while to find my way here. When the ship I escaped my old life on made its final port, I journeyed from town to town, exploring what each one had to offer. It was nice being able to pick up and leave whenever I wanted. It was the freedom I desired so much as a young girl.

But then, five years ago, I craved routine—acceptance—so I decided to settle down in this small town and lead a quiet, solitary life.

During the day, I spend most of my time inside the tiny cottage I bought with the last of the gold coins gifted to me all those years ago. I have a small garden I tend to before the winter freezes all my sweet-smelling plants and herbs. A few creatures from the neighboring forest will stumble onto my lawn, and I always leave out little treats for them. I'll never forget the baby deer that ate half my herb garden and was sick for nearly a week.

The poor darling did pull through after I spent many nights hand-feeding her.

The doe's mother had come to collect her from *The Woods,* and I watched the pair trot off happily. The vastness of that sprawling tangle of trees and overgrown grass doesn't scare me —not as it once did. All my visitors from there are sweet animals—if they can survive there, surely nothing too evil lurks within.

After spending my day toiling away in my garden or reading one of the countless novels I've collected over my travels, I can be found here at the Wolf's Fang once the sun sets. For being the only tavern in Moon's Hollow, it is a relatively peaceful establishment. We rarely get visitors from other settlements this far north, which I am grateful for.

Old Bill, who runs this tavern, is a kind man with warm brown eyes and a graying beard. He let me rent out a room above the Wolf's Fang before I purchased my cottage. He's kept my pay consistent over these five years. The concept of having my own money is still new to me. As a princess, the idea of working for money was an insult. Now, it's become my biggest blessing.

It's given me my autonomy, and I'm grateful for it.

Yet, even as I delight in all the freedom I've experienced, something has shifted in me recently: a desire to belong to someone—not in the way I belonged to my parents or as a prisoner to the loveless marriage they would've forced me into— but to make a life with someone of my choosing.

I rarely think about the past these days. I had become so absorbed in my new, fast-paced life that I seldom had the chance to. The last time I heard anything about my former life was a few whispered rumors shortly after I arrived about some royal guards being spotted to the south. They were still looking for a missing princess, but after five years, no one had much hope she would be found.

I had nodded at the patrons who brought the gossip, refilled their cups, and spent the night wide awake, thinking it wouldn't be long until I was found. However, they never came. No one has mentioned even a passing whisper of my parents. This far out of their kingdom, I am far beyond their reach.

Shaking myself from the dark turn of my thoughts, I pick up a discarded silver mug and polish it with a clean rag. The past will drown me if I let it. I am safe here—life is simple. Tonight is a testament to that.

A few patrons are sipping mugs of ale along the polished wooden bar. Their crumpled clothes and the dirt caked under their nails indicate they spent all day tending to the fields. An older couple plays a game of cards at one of the small tables near the roaring fireplace. The red bricks glow from the crackling hearth. Above it sits the stuffed head of a stag, its proud horns nearly brushing the low beams of the ceiling.

I wrinkle my nose at the decor before returning to the mug in my hand.

A smattering of voices can be heard just beyond the tavern door. I look up just in time to see the creaky door fly open and bang against the stone wall. My stomach sinks when I realize who's walked in.

Timson's dark eyes find me in an instant. Licking his lips, he gives me a saccharine grin before advancing towards the bar. Tonight, he's flanked by six of his lackeys, each staring at him like he is a god. They worship him as one, as do most of the people in this town. Being the most proficient hunter in the county will inspire that sort of treatment.

Me, on the other hand? I can't stand the man.

He is the one sore spot in my otherwise idyllic, if mundane, life. His wandering eyes and hands are well-known amongst the women here. Since working in the Wolf's Fang, I've had the unfortunate pleasure of catching his eye and being extremely accessible.

A fact he's well aware of as he stalks toward me. His dark hair is pulled back in a low bun. His temples are beginning to gray—the scar running from his left brow to his cheek glints in the low candlelight. Timson would be handsome if his eyes didn't betray the malice simmering within his soul.

They are unkind—ruthless—just like the man himself.

His well-made clothes are wrinkled and covered in dark stains, indicating that he and the others have just returned from a hunt. One of the other men has a white bandage tied around his lower leg and walks with a distinct limp. The others seem in much better condition by comparison.

He comes to stand on the other side of the bar, and I've never been more grateful for the old wooden beam. Timson bangs his meaty fist on the bar before dropping a fist full of gold coins onto the polished surface. They hit with soft thuds and sparkle brilliantly. His thin lips pull into a grin that makes my skin crawl.

"A round of ale for me and my hunting party, beauty."

I try not to recoil at the nickname as I scoop up the coins. Somehow, I keep my hands steady as I ready their drinks. The thick foam atop their mugs glistens as I set them before the group. Each one is snatched and drunk down almost instantly —except Timson, who looks at me expectantly. Suppressing my urge to groan, I know what he's waiting for.

Looking at each man more closely, I see how disheveled they are. Sweat still clings to their brows, and a few have fresh-looking scratches along their hands and cheeks. Holes decorate a few of their trousers and coats. My eyes return to Timson, whose grin deepens. Picking up my rag and discarded mug, I go back to polishing while trying to keep my voice as casual as possible.

"Good hunting?"

Timson nods, taking a large gulp of his ale.

"You could say that," he says, pining me with a look as he licks the foam from his unkempt beard. "Killing is when a man is most in control—the state in which we were meant to show our unparalleled prowess. That is why you should accompany me as requested—it is a privilege to bear witness to one as exceptional as myself in that state, I'm told."

I smile politely and avert my gaze to the mug in my hand. It's a wonder I haven't rubbed off its silver coating.

"I'm afraid I don't have the stomach for such things, sir. I barely eat meat as it is. Therefore, I don't think—"

"I am well aware of your peculiar tastes, Stella."

My name upon his lips causes my stomach to churn. I don't have to look up to know his eyes have narrowed. Clearly, he is recalling the times he's left boar meat at my door, and I let it go rotten before some other predator drug it away. You would think after the tenth time, a man would get the hint that his *gifts* were not wanted.

"Well," I say, hoping to end this interaction for the evening. "I am pleased you all returned safely from your excursion."

The lie tastes like bile, but I swallow it down.

"He's being modest," one of Timson's lackeys—Jaq—says and claps him on the back.

I somehow manage not to roll my eyes—modest is one of the last words I'd use to describe Timson. This tavern and the one time I had the unfortunate pleasure of glimpsing his home are littered with his hunting trophies. How can one live surrounded by so much death?

"We captured a demon," Jaq continues.

"A beast—you wouldn't believe the size of," another voice chimes in—Henri.

"Men," Timson says, "I'm sure the lady isn't interested in the extraordinary details of our hunt. We nearly lost our lives out there when I stared down the muzzle of that creature."

My brows lower, but Timson clasps his mug in his hand and turns to his hunting party.

"To the devils that walk upright like men. May their heads always find themselves mounted on my walls."

The group of men bang their mugs together in a hearty cheer. Frothy ale slips over the sides and splatters onto the top of the bar. Setting down my clean mug, I push up on my toes to wipe up the mess they've made on the wooden top. Timson stares at me over the lip of his mug—I can feel his eyes like a caress.

Before I register his movements, his hand comes down atop mine, trapping me. My head snaps up as the ale-soaked rag wets my palm. His dark eyes rove over me, openly appraising the curve of my waist and the neckline of my gown. It is modest, and yet his stare makes me feel naked—I itch to find another layer to cover myself so there is no skin for his eyes to behold.

"You know," he purrs, loud enough for his hunting party to hear, "I've been thinking about how unsafe your cottage is. All alone in *The Woods*—it's not a place for a lone woman."

I give him my most gracious smile—an expression I've mastered during interactions such as these. Gently, I pull my hand back, wanting to scrub the skin raw and remove the feel of his calloused fingers atop mine.

"Thank you for your concern, sir, but I like my cottage."

Timson's lips tighten.

"Something awful could happen to you, and no one is there to help." He takes a sip from his mug, setting it with a thud atop the bar. "You should come live with me."

His offer rips breath from his lungs. He has been forward

before, but this is something new. The room feels too small as if the walls are pressing in on me.

Timson seems not to notice my rigid posture as he continues.

"After my wife's death, I need someone tending to my children. Childbirth fever took her before she could give me the ten that I wanted." He grins, showing me his yellowed teeth. Clearly, the memory of his deceased wife is not a sad one. "Besides, a woman as pretty as you shouldn't work. I can provide for you."

My mouth goes dry. It feels as if I've swallowed poison. Beyond my churning stomach, my hands tremble as they ring in front of my white apron. Children with Timson? I couldn't think of a worse fate. No, I won't even consider such a thing.

I have not come this far only to end up in a loveless pairing with a man I despise. My lips part as if to tell him as much—summoning all the courage I have to do so—when, as if by magic, Old Bill appears next to me behind the bar. Dropping off a fresh set of mugs, his wrinkled fingers gently push them toward me. His brown eyes sparkle behind the thick rims of his round glasses.

"What is this I hear about devils?" he asks, the wrinkles on his face pulling tight as he raises a gray brow.

I sigh and try not to sag with relief as Old Bill stands before me, partially blocking me from the other man.

Timson's eyes narrow, but he steps back from the bar. This unfortunate conversation has been put to rest, at least for tonight. However, I know it won't be long before he broaches the topic again, and I'll have to give my answer.

"A few farmers have reported their sheep being slaughtered," Timson explains. "Reports of them waking up in the morning to find the half-eaten corpses of their flock rotting in their yards."

My stomach twists, but Old Bill merely nods.

"I've heard a few complaining about such things these past few weeks. Wolf?"

"A demon," Jaq interrupts, slamming his mug down on the bar.

Sliding me a gold coin, I quickly refill his ale.

"A demon?" Old Bill's lips pull into a frown.

"A demon," Jaq repeats. "Without Timson, we'd surely be dead."

The praise brings a self-indulgent smile to Timson's face. It's as if I can see his ego expand and fill the room—sucking the air from it and choking us all with his self-importance.

"Our tale is interesting, Old Bill," Timson sighs. "Three days and nights, we scoured the land for any hints of the creature killing the sheep. Now we know we weren't dealing with any simple beast. A tricky demon it was, but ultimately no match for a hunter such as myself."

A round of cheers goes up as Timson lavishes another heated look at me. I couldn't be any less impressed if I tried.

"There were no tracks to follow—even the dogs couldn't get a proper scent that didn't lead us to a dead end. We thought all was lost until I finally found something that put us on its trail."

"No one but Timson would've spotted it," chirps Henri.

"Just near the edge of *The Woods*, I found it. A few drops of red blood clinging to the grass lead us directly to it—holding the quivering body of a tawny-colored doe to its mouth."

My head snaps up.

"Holding it?" I ask. Old Bill throws me a perplexed look.

Timson nods. "Yes, holding it. It stood upright like a man—bigger than any bear I've seen. It was a creature from legend and nightmare. When I finally trained my rifle on it, the creature dropped the deer and turned its glowing eyes on us. There was no warning before it pounced and sank his claw in Bron's leg."

The man I noticed earlier with the limp raises his mug and pats the stained bandage around his calf.

"Saved my life—Timson did."

Timson shrugs, but the dismissive movement is just for show. He delights in their praise and attention. Indeed, the whole tavern has stopped its chatter to listen to his tale.

"I only came prepared for the hunt. My daddy always told me never to leave the house without his sacred bullets—ones made of pure silver."

The mug Old Bill is polishing falls onto the bartop.

"You don't mean what I think you do—surely not Timson? And you've captured such a creature? A—"

"A wolfman," Timson answers for him. "It's chained up with heavy metal shackles behind the old mill at the edge of town. The beast is riddled with enough silver to keep it weak. The bear trap through its back leg will also stop any escape attempts."

A wolfman? Of course, I've heard the legends of such creatures since I arrived in this town. I assumed they were merely stories—tales used on naughty children to get them to behave. Now Timson claims he's captured one and is keeping it tied up? Whatever poor creature he's taken is undoubtedly suffering in the dark—cold and alone.

The thought makes my chest ache.

"In the morning, we'll skin him. His pelt should fetch a nice price."

The wooden floor feels unstable beneath my feet. Dizziness washes over me as I grip the bar's edge for support. Nausea swims up from my stomach and dampens my brow.

"I'll bring you its head, Old Bill. Mount it here as another trophy in my honor."

"A wolfman, truly?" Old Bill's voice is soft. "There hasn't been a sighting of one in decades—most of us believe them to be just myths."

Timson waves a dismissive hand.

"You can investigate it for yourself, old man. For now, I want to celebrate being alive with another pint of ale."

He produces another gold coin and pushes his empty mug towards me. My clammy hand extends toward it, but Old Bill intercepts me. He pushes back Timson's coin before reaching beneath the bar and pulling out an entire bottle of whiskey. The amber liquid swishes behind the thick glass.

Handing it to Timson, Old Bill says, "For keeping the town safe, why don't you and your hunters treat yourselves? On the house."

Timson nods his thanks as Old Bill turns towards me.

"Stella, get our friends here some glasses."

My hands feel numb as I reach below the bartop to locate them. The other hunters have gathered at a far table, and soon, only Old Bill, Timson, and I are gathered around the bar. Most of the other patrons have left for the evening, having had their fill of the hunters' tale.

"Don't forget a glass for yourself, beauty. We should all celebrate that this beast didn't get the chance to eat us."

I nod, unable to even form one of my fake smiles. My hands knock into a few glasses beneath the bar. I'm afraid I'll drop them due to my sweaty palms.

There's a creature out there confined and scared—suffering. Its death is looming at the hands of such cruel captors. Perhaps it is misplaced, but I can't help but feel a kinship towards the chained beast. Was I not once just like it? Kept against my will as my future was torn away?

The thought of any creature suffering has never sat well with me, but this feels different. It is as if my very soul is compelling me to act. But what would I do? What *could* I do?

I set the glasses in front of Timson, who fills one up partially with amber liquid and pushes it towards me. I stare at the glass, my reflection faint in the sparkling liquid. Leaning over the bar to collect the rest of the glasses, Timson's voice is a low caress.

"Join us by the fire, Stella. We didn't get to finish our earlier conversation."

Taking the glass, I try a sip of the whiskey. It burns down my throat before settling in my riotous stomach. The pain allows me to refocus and kindle my resolve. I am not as helpless as I once was. An act of kindness saved me, and I will be damned if I do not repay it to another in need.

"I'm sorry, Timson," I say, knowing how much he likes it when I use his name. "The washing up still needs to be done."

The hunter looks displeased, but remembering the free whiskey in his arms, he turns on a booted heel toward his men. They pat him on the back and cheer; soon, they are lost to their cups. Timson throws me one final look over his shoulder.

"You cannot avoid me or this conversation forever, Stella."

Icy nails drag up my spine as I collect discarded mugs from the top of the bar. Old Bill lingers behind me as I gather a soapy water basin and begin cleaning.

"There are worse husbands than Timson, Stella. Someone like him could keep you safe—especially alone in that cottage."

I barely glance up from my washing, my voice a whisper.

"But who would keep me safe from Timson?"

Old Bill huffs humorlessly and begins drying the clean mugs beside me.

"I just worry about you—I have since you started here. Stella, you're a hard worker, but this is no life for a young woman."

His statement is from a place of concern, but it stings just the same. It seems that no matter how you are born in life—a princess or a peasant—women are constantly forced into roles that men believe are fitting for us.

Do I want a family? Yes, I always have. However, I want one with someone of my choosing. I will not bind myself to a man because this village believes I must. I will not marry or have children with anyone I do not love.

"I can take care of myself, Old Bill. I have been doing so for a very long time." I hand him the final clean mug and wipe off the bar's surface. "It is not my plan to work here forever—I want a family—but not with someone like Timson."

Old Bill raises a brow. "Well, we don't get many handsome strangers passing through. I fear, my dear, your options here are becoming slim."

I merely shrug. "It'll work out—somehow, things in my life always do."

Old Bill chuckles as he asks, "Magic?"

A secret smile curls my lips. "Maybe."

Old Bill laughs again and settles the final mug below the bar. My eyes drift to the hunters around the fire. The orange light paints them in jagged shadows. The bottle is half empty, and they'll be severely drunk by the time they are done. It is usually up to me to close up, and I don't have a particular interest in being around here once they run out of liquor.

Old Bill follows my stare.

"Why don't you head home early," he says as if reading my thoughts. "I have a feeling those hunters will want to sleep here, and they won't take too kindly to you trying to kick them out."

"Thank you," I say, kissing his old, wrinkled cheek.

Hanging up my apron behind the bar, I quickly collect my simple cloak and leather satchel before taking one final look at the hunters. The cruel gleam in their eyes as they dramatically reenact their hunt makes my blood boil. I decide immediately what I must do, and there is no time to waste.

I hope I can get it done while they're all still nursing their sore heads in the morning. Snagging something I need from the bartop unnoticed, I head to the door quickly and plunge into the night.

2

———

STELLA

The cold night air whips around me, and I pull my cloak tighter.

Looming up ahead is the old mill, its large wheel unmoving even with the strong wind. The journey from the tavern had been quick enough. The closer I crept to my destination, I could hear low hums of pain. Whatever is chained behind the crumbling building is clearly injured.

Its soft, keening sounds slice through my heart.

After hearing how the bar patrons talk about wolfmen, I'm a bit wary of what I'll find up ahead. Regardless, this poor thing needs my help, and I will give it. If anyone besides Timson said it was dangerous, I might believe them. However, just because it comes from *The Woods* does not mean it's evil.

That's my hope at least. All I can do is offer up a prayer that it doesn't turn on me the moment I appear.

The sounds of suffering get louder as I cut through the overgrown grass. This part of town is deserted. No one was on the street when I started this way, but I'll have to be quick. The old mill sits below a hill, which is easy to happen upon, and I don't want word of what I'm doing getting back to Timson.

I shudder to think about his reaction to finding out what I'm doing.

My hand wraps tightly around the barely touched glass of whiskey I took from the bar. I hope Old Bill won't notice the glass missing until I can return it tomorrow.

Rounding the corner, my steps falter at what I find.

There he is. Tide to a post with a heavy iron chain wrapped around his throat. He is larger than any man I've seen—any animal either. The scent of blood is heavy in the air. His breathing is ragged. The thick muscles of his shoulders and chest rise and fall. The wind whips at his black fur, causing him to shiver more intensely.

His pointed ears drop down as he curls further in towards himself. My eyes trail his muscled frame, registering his sharp claws before glimpsing his calf. My breath catches at the gruesome sight. A bear trap has punctured through the lower half of his leg. It will be a wonder if the bone isn't broken. The brown grass around him is soaked with his blood.

I stumble back a step, accidentally stepping on a fallen stick. The loud snap alerts the beast. His massive head whips towards me. With my position revealed, I have no choice but to show myself. A low growl emanates from him, his sharp fangs flashing in the moonlight.

My heart pounds and my mouth goes dry. Perhaps this wasn't my best idea, but I've come too far to turn back now. Somewhere deep inside me, a voice whispers that everything will be okay and not to be afraid. My intuition hasn't failed me yet, and I just have to hope tonight won't be the first time it does.

Another low growl echoes around me. Sliding its thickly corded arms back, I watch its eyes peel open. My whiskey glass nearly slides from my hand as our gazes lock. His eyes are golden, like the throne my father once sat on. Even in the dim light, the shimmer. Only that's not what steals my breath.

These are not a beast's eyes but a man's—human eyes stare back at me, untrusting and filled with pain. My heart starts to ache even more. As our eyes stay on each other, I watch the tenseness in his body dissipate before he lets out a soft whimper.

Glancing behind me, I make sure no one else is about one last time before walking closer to the chained creature. The beast shivers at my approach, tugging on the metal restraints with a loud clang.

"Shh," I say softly. "I'm not going to hurt you."

Kneeling next to him, he smells like pine and smoke. Then, the nauseating metallic scent of blood stings my nostrils. Glancing down, I can see the damage to his leg. The metal prongs are rusted and protrude at odd angles through the muscle of his calf. Clumps of black fur and flesh cling to the old trap. The wound will surely fester if not tended to properly.

Carefully, I set my whiskey down and remove the bag slung over my shoulder. Tentatively, I reach out, only to be met with a soft snarl. My eyes connect with his once more as I will him to see me not as a threat. Just because the streets are bare now does not mean they will remain so—I won't be able to help him if they put me in chains, too.

"This is gonna hurt." My hand touches the soft fur of his leg, and he whimpers. "I'm going to try and free you from this."

The wolfman's eyes close as he lets out a harsh sigh, which I take as his consent to do what I must.

Touching the cold metal of the trap, I feel around, trying not to gag at the wet, sticky blood coating my hands. I'll need to do this fast to minimize damage. Taking a deep breath, my fingers wrap around both sets of metal teeth.

Without warning, I rip them apart and free the creature's leg.

A loud growl tears through the night, swallowing up the audible groan of the metal trap. Moving quickly, I pick up my glass of whiskey and promptly douse his leg before he can pull it back. I'll have to find a way to clean it thoroughly. Blood gushes from the wound, but luckily, the bone does not appear broken.

The wolfman lets out a harsh snarl as I reach into my bag and pull out a few rolls of clean cloths I took from the tavern. Dabbing at his wound, the first towel is quickly saturated with crimson. Gently, I tie the next one above his wound to slow the blood flow. I learned how to do this during my travels— knowing the skills of a healer would come in handy one day.

I never would've imagined using them to treat a wolfman.

"I'm sorry," I whisper. "You have to be in a lot of pain. This will have to do until I can tend to your wound properly."

His ears lower as he pushes up on his forearms. The muscles bulge beneath his fur as those golden eyes find mine again. Despite the fur, the ears, and, of course, the snout, he seems incredibly human. My stomach flutters under his intense gaze, but I can't look away.

"Can you understand me?"

He blinks once before lowering his head.

"Good, I'm going to unchain you now."

Again, he merely blinks at me, but I take that as agreement. Rising on my feet, I circle behind him. Tethered to the post is a snarl of chains. Timson and his hunters took their time to ensure the wolfman would not escape. Iron chains wrap around his ankles and wrists. They are secured with a heavy metal lock at the back of the post. The chain around his neck is bound in the same way.

Sighing, I look around for anything useful. I should've tried to snag Timson's keys, but that would've required getting closer to him than I could stomach. Instead, my eyes land on a large rock. Wrinkling my nose, I bend down to retrieve it. It is not the best, but it is better than nothing.

Raising the rock, I quickly bring it down on the old iron locks. The bang echoes around us, and I pause, listening for the footsteps of anyone who may have heard the noise. When everything remains still, I repeat the process: Bang. Pause. Bang. Pause.

The first lock to give way is the one securing his ankles. Once they fall loose, he growls, flexes his muscles, and whimpers as he tries to put any weight on his injured leg.

Sparks fly as I hammer away on the next lock. After what feels like hours, it is dented enough to fall loose, and the chains around his wrists sag. With a snarl, he claws at the iron binding his neck and yanks, the metal turning to shreds in his hands as he removes his final restraint.

Rising swiftly and favoring his uninjured leg, the creature towers over me. He blocks out the moon as he rises to his full height. I take him in, my heart pounding against my ribs. His powerful chest and abdomen give way to thick thighs. Dark fur that I know feels incredibly soft is matted with blood in certain places. The bullet holes Timson put through him are leaking blood in a steady stream.

I don't let my eyes drift any lower than his waist, trying to ignore the heat creeping up my cheeks.

He is handsome. The revelation shocks me like falling into a pool of cold water. He is a beast—yet his eyes tell a different story. They reveal the hidden depths of his soul, and it calls to me. The rock slides from my hand and hits the ground with a thud. His eyes drift towards it before returning to my face.

I fight to hide my shiver as they slide over every inch of my body. When Timson did it early, I felt nothing but disgust, but with this wolfman, all I feel is warmth. Perhaps I have genuinely lost all semblance of sense after all this time.

The wolfman inhales deeply, his nostrils flaring. I lick over my dry lips before opening my mouth. Before I can say anything, a sound echoes from down the road. In the silence of the night, it becomes clear in a moment. My stomach drops.

It's Timson and his hunters. Their voices slurred from drink as they stumble up the path towards us. The wolfman turns towards the sound, his lips peeling back from his teeth in a snarl. His body is tense as he lowers to a crouching potion.

"Go human," he snarls without looking at me.

His voice sends shivers down my spine. It is rough and inviting at the same time. I wish to drink the sound down. Again, I must question if I have truly gone mad.

The voices get closer as another breeze picks up. My hair flies in front of my face. I watch the wolfman scent the air again, his muscles softening, if only for a moment.

"Wait," I urge, watching him coil for the attack again. "You are in no shape to take them on—even as drunk as they are, especially not with those bullets still in you. I need to remove them and clean the wounds. Come with me, or you risk getting an infection."

The wolfman snaps his head towards me as his ears flatten. Lowering himself to all fours, he stalks towards me with a noticeable limp. He stops, his nose pressing against my stomach before rising once more. His claws gently trace my sides. A gasp slips from my lips.

I've never felt like this before. The fluttering in my stomach has moved lower—a dull ache beginning to intensify.

"How do I know you aren't planning to kill me?" he purrs softly. His head lowers as he skims his velvety nose up my neck. "What if this is all some trick—those hunters sending me someone as delicious as you to lower my guard? It'd make killing me easier."

My eyes fall shut as he nuzzles against my collarbone. His fur skims over my exposed skin, causing goosebumps to rise. Somehow, I manage to find my voice.

"It's no trick," I sigh. "I just want to help you."

I feel his body shift away from me. Blinking my heavy-lidded eyes, I watch as he tries to put more weight on his leg. He whimpers as the voices of the hunters get closer. Luckily, their drunken stupor has slowed their ability to travel. Still, they'll be here soon if we don't hurry.

"Come with me," I say, touching his arm. Soft fur kisses my fingertips.

I don't fear him—a revelation more shocking than finding him attractive. For some reason, despite his evident ability to cause me harm at the flick of his wrist, I know he won't hurt me. That will not be the case for the hunters should they happen upon us.

"My cottage isn't far from here. I can guide us there, but we must go before they see us."

The wolfman blinks at me before opening his mouth. A voice cuts him off before I can hear what I'm sure will be another protest.

"Let's skin him now," a male voice cheers—Jaq.

"Yes!" A smattering of voices rises in agreement.

The wolfman tenses as my heart continues to pound. Sweat glides down my spine.

"I'll skin him, boys, use the money from his pelt to woo that stubborn barmaid. I know her cunt is tighter than anything," laughs Timson.

My hands feel numb, and my knees threaten to buckle. Bile coats my tongue at his crude words.

"If you marry her, you'll let us have a turn, won't you?" a familiar voice—Henri—asks.

"Only once I've broken her in."

The world around me shifts and tilts. I reach out to steady myself on the post—vile, wretched man. I cannot marry him. I won't. I'd rather slit my own throat. He thinks he hunts beasts for sport, but no creature is as wretched and monstrous as him.

A low growl cuts through the air as the wolfman's eyes burn into mine.

"Please," I say weakly. "If they find out I freed you—"

I can't even bring myself to complete the sentence.

Rolling his massive shoulders, the wolfman inclines his head in agreement. I try not to sag with relief as I quickly gather my things, leaving no trace of our existence.

"My home is just over that hill—nestled right into *The Woods*."

Footsteps sound from near the front of the mill. We'll have to be run, and I've never been particularly—

The wolfman walks over to me before lowering to all fours again. Dipping his head in front of me, I'm unsure what he is offering. Then it clicks—he wants me to climb onto his back.

"Are you sure? Your injury—"

But a loud retching sound from just around the corner stops my protest. A few voices jeer at Henri for being unable to handle his liquor.

This may be our only chance of escaping unseen. Quickly, I grab his fur and hoist myself atop his muscled back. My dress rips in the process, but I pay little mind to it. My thighs go to either side of him, his fur tickling my most tender flesh. He is wide enough that the muscles of my legs burn with the stretch. Leaning down, I hold tight to his powerful frame.

With a loud howl, the beast below me leaps forward and takes off into the night. Darkness swallows us up as I hear Timson's yell pierce through the air. I pay it no mind and only hold on tighter to the wolfman.

He runs without stopping, even if I know his injury must be hurting him. The grassy terrain of the village is a blur as we race towards my home. There is determination lacing through every powerful stride. His body absorbs the impact as we travel faster and faster. I've never experienced anything like it.

I recall the harsh set of his muscles when he heard Timson's and the other's voices. Despite his wounds, he was ready to take them head-on. It stands to reason that for the first time since coming to this village, there may finally be someone who wants Timson dead as much as I do.

3

STELLA

Coming to a stop outside my tiny cottage, I slide from the wolfman's back.

My modest home has a simple thatch roof and plain stone walls. A small herb garden is nestled along one side, while the back leads directly into *The Woods*. It's quiet this far away from Moon's Hollow. The sound of rustling leaves and hooting owls breaks the late-night silence. The large moon is our only light source, casting everything in hazy blue light.

I turn to look at my companion. His golden eyes are guarded, casting me wary glances as he scents the air. Looking behind his shoulder, his pointed ears twitch before lowering. I wait to hear raised voices coming from the village, indicating that Timson and his men saw us, but all remains quiet. After a moment, his eyes return to mine expectantly.

Reaching into my bag, I produce my iron house key and quickly unlock the front door. The old metal hinges squeak open. The front part of my home is a basic kitchen with a circular table and two chairs resting against the wall. Off to the right is my sitting area, where a small loveseat sits next to a side table. A few dogeared books are strewn across the cushions. My wooden bookshelf is nearly buckling from the heavy tomes stacked on each shelf. Behind a curtain is my bedroom, which has a bed and a small wardrobe.

It's far more modest than the castle I grew up in, but it's mine. This was the first place I ever felt truly free and safe. Even as I hear the wolfman slide over the threshold and the door slam shut behind him, I still feel secure. While the danger he presents is obvious, I don't fear him.

Turning towards him, I gesture towards the small table with the matching wooden chairs.

"Have a seat there while I go and fetch my supplies."

Golden eyes narrow in on me, but he remains silent. His massive body settles atop the chair. It groans under his weight. Somehow he manages to suck all the air from the room and make my cottage feel ten times smaller. My eyes dip to the matted dark hair of his chest and the oily sheen of blood on his fur. Hanging my bag from a peg at the door, I open the cupboards in my kitchen to collect what I need.

The first place I found refuge after leaving my parents' home was with an old healer. She taught me basic herbology and medicinal purposes for easy-to-grow plants. I've been honing this skill these last few years. I'm not an experienced healer, but I know enough to be useful. If I can get the bullets out, I should be able to clean his wounds enough for them to begin healing.

Plucking a box of matches from the drawer, I light the large pillar candle on my table to illuminate the space. I lay out a stack of clean cloth and a few herbs to slow the bleeding. Taking my small metal tongs, I dunk them into cleaning alcohol and turn towards the wolfman.

"Where did they shoot you?" I ask.

For a moment, I believe he won't answer me. His human eyes swirl with a dozen questions. His lips twitch as if fighting not to snarl. Flaring his nostrils, he shakes himself before raising a large hand. He touches two spots on his chest where his fur is the most matted, then drops his hand lower along his hip. Crimson stains the simple cloth covering his legs to just below the knees.

I nod, swallowing once and then slowly approaching with my tongs extended. He is just like anyone else—any other man—only a bit more hairy. Still, I have a job to do despite my racing heart. The scent of pine invades my lungs as I lean down. My hand tangles in the warm fur of his chest. It's softer than silk, and I wonder how it would feel along my body.

My face warms at the thought, and I remind myself again to focus.

"This is going to hurt," I warn.

With a steady hand, I locate the first bullet wound. The wolfman barely whimpers as my tongs lock around the silver and tug it free. The wound steams—his body rejecting the metal. Luckily, it wasn't too deep of a wound. I drop the metal into a glass. My fingers are stained with blood as I gently part the hair over the other wound.

Locking my tongs around the piece of metal, I'm so focused that I barely register his soft voice.

"Why?"

I glance up at him and nearly melt from the intensity of his stare. The deep sound of his voice dances along my skin and sinks into my bones. It's a pleasant sound, even if it is edged in pain.

Licking my lips, my eyes lower back to his wound.

"Why what?" I ask.

"Why help me?"

With a gentle tug, I remove the second bullet and drop it into the glass. Blood pours from the wound and onto my fingers. With the two on his chest removed, I douse a cloth in antiseptic and press it into the openings. He gives a muffled groan as I apply pressure.

Looking up, I meet his eyes once more.

"I can't watch someone suffer when I have the means to help." I remove the red stained cloth and apply a fresh one. "Someone showed me kindness when I needed it the most. This is my way of repaying it."

Directing him to hold the cloth, I lower beside him and untangle the mass of dark fur at his hip. Blood makes my fingers slippery as I part the sodden strands. Finally, my fingers brush the hole. A few inches higher, and it would've struck his hip bone. This wound is deeper, and he squirms as I push my tongs into the opening.

"Have you always been like this?" I ask, trying to distract him and out of curiosity. It's less tense when he's speaking to me, and I want to know more about him.

His whole body tightens, and I feel his eyes upon me like a touch.

"A monster, you mean?" he snarls. "I know the stories you humans tell of my kind. Animals slain for our pelts, our heads mounted as trophies."

I swallow as bile races up my throat.

"I've never much cared for animal pelts," I say, trying to keep my voice light. "Not when silk is so much nicer."

My tongs lock around the final bullet and tug. A growl leaves his lips before breaking off in a whimper. I gently rock and tug the piece of metal before pulling it free. Fresh blood spills from the opening and soaks the cloth of his shorts. Setting my tongs down, I grab a fresh cloth and drench it with more antiseptic. Reaching towards his wound, his hand encircles my wrist, stopping me.

"There are more of my kind out there," he says. "We are born—not made. My father was a wolfman. My mother was a human."

I nod. His palm on my skin makes my blood heat. After a

moment, he releases me, and I press the cloth to his wound. A low hiss leaves him.

"Do you all live nearby? Is that how the hunters found you?"

"No," he rasps. "I was traveling alone."

I nod and quickly change the cloth to a fresh one.

"What about you?" he asks.

I shrug, a familiar ache forming in my chest.

"No family," I say simply.

"Do you have a mate?"

I lower my brows. "Like a husband? No."

His golden eyes seem to darken, and I feel heat climb up my cheeks. This wolfman has no problem being direct. Perhaps he was worried about a spouse coming home and finding his wife tending to a creature from *The Woods*, but he does not need to worry about that.

"Timson—one of the hunters who found you—has made me several marriage offers." I don't know why I'm sharing this with him, perhaps because I know he and I hold the same disdain for that repulsive man. "But I would rather take my chances with—"

"A wild beast?" he supplies.

I'm blushing in earnest now as I nod.

"Well, now that you aren't growling at me, you don't seem so bad."

His lips twitch, and I don't think it's a snarl he's trying to suppress this time.

"You don't know anything about me." His ears lower. "What is your name, human?"

"Stella," I say softly. "And yours."

"Ciaryn."

I nod, rising to my feet. "It's nice to meet you, Ciaryn."

Together, we work silently to bind the wounds on his chest and hip. It takes most of my clean cloth to wrap around his massive frame. Once I am satisfied with the dressing, I apply the same antiseptic solution to his leg where the trap had broken through the skin. Once it is bound, I return to the kitchen table and begin making a concoction to treat any lingering infection.

I extend a glass of dark liquid towards him. With a sniff, he rears back.

"This will stop any of your wounds from festering. Drink it."

Reluctantly, he takes it from my hands. He sips it before shaking his head.

"All of it," I command.

With a deep sigh, he drinks down the whole elixir before grimacing. I take the glass from his hand and glance out the window. The night is still, and a few fireflies dance along the overgrown grass of my front lawn.

"You should spend the night here. They're likely prowling the town and forest for you, and you're in no condition to travel. The dose I gave you was potent, and you'll be feeling tired." I gesture towards my small bedroom. "You take the bed; it should be able to fit you."

Ciaryn shakes his head.

"The floor is fine."

"Nonsense," I say, waving a dismissive hand. "You need to rest for your wounds to heal. In the morning, I'll change your bandages."

Brushing past him to turn down the bed, his hand snags my wrist again. This close, we are eye to eye. The warmth of his body soaks into me. Pine seeps through the overwhelming scent of blood. His touch is gentle.

"Thank you," he says. "Your kindness won't be forgotten, Stella."

A fresh blush dances across my cheeks as I nod. Ciaryn's eyes droop, and I help him from the chair towards the bed. Once we reach it, he falls backward onto the covers. The wooden frame creaks but holds firm. It's not long before his eyes fall shut, and his breathing turns deep and even.

With a sigh, I turn back towards the kitchen and wash the blood from my hands. My dress is stained, and I don't have the energy to do much more than unlace it and discard it with my boots. Dressed only in my cotton shift, I find an old blanket draped along the arm of the couch and settle onto the worn cushions.

It's not too uncomfortable. My neck will be stiff in the morning, but it's only for one night. I should feel uneasy at the creature occupying my bed, but I feel entirely safe. It's an odd realization but not an unpleasant one.

With exhaustion weighing me down, I let the darkness pull me into a deep, dreamless sleep.

4

CIARYN

This human is different.

She is kind—something I've never experienced from her kind. While she had every reason to fear me, she treated me with compassion. With my advanced healing, the wounds along my chest and hip are nearly healed. The skin of my calf has knitted back together, and my muscles are strong again.

Stella is brave for such a small thing—not many humans would risk freeing a beast like me from their shackles and rendering aid.

Her strength steals my breath. Curled up on her small couch, she looks impossibly fragile. The dark, golden strands of her hair fan across the pale cushions. Her freckled cheeks are dusted with pink. Delicate snores whistle from her tiny nose. The sun begins to rise and paints her in its warm light. The first rays of dawn had stirred me from the sedative she administered.

I haven't slept that well in a long time. There is comfort in her presence, not to mention her delicious scent, which coats everything inside this small cottage. Stella smells of honey and wildflowers.

Now, I realize it had been her scent that brought me to this village. I had caught a whiff of it on the wind while running. It stopped me dead in my tracks and tugged me closer to this settlement. The scent had consumed me in a way I didn't understand. I was so enthralled in finding its source that I hadn't noticed the hunters had spotted my trail.

If I hadn't been distracted, they never would've captured me. I have half a mind to track them down this morning and to gut them for what they did.

But more than anything, I wish to find the one called Timson and shred him alive for daring to covet Stella as his bride. I understand the male's desire for her—I feel it now as I stare down at her. Her beauty is otherworldly.

Even though I shouldn't disturb her, I can't help but run a claw over her round cheek. Her smooth skin is warm—softer than the petals of a rose. I wonder if she is this soft everywhere. Before I do something foolish, I pull my hand back. I need to leave before I bring any trouble to her door, not to mention the obligations I must return to.

The familiar ache yawns open in my chest.

Damn my father for leaving me. Damn the hunters who killed my mother and severed whatever long life she and my father would have shared. After she was gone, he was never the same—each day without her was agony. Now that he has passed, I hope their reunion was all he dreamed it would be.

I am not fit to be alpha. What kind of leader abandons their pack the way I have? I have to face them before too much more time passes. Still, my blood heats at the idea of revenge. The hunters who killed my mother were dealt with long ago, and my mouth waters at the thought of eradicating even more.

As I stare down at Stella, I realize I must leave. Despite a part of me wanting to remain for another night, the longer I linger here, the more likely I'll be found out. I must get as far away from here as possible. It's the only way to keep her safe. For her kindness, I'll leave her village in peace.

Still, I continue to watch her slumber. I can't take my eyes off of her. I drink her in, letting her sweet scent fill my lungs. I don't understand this pull I feel towards her—at least, that's what I tell myself. Considering what it means would make this situation all the more dire. I cannot allow myself to be overcome by the rampant desire pounding in my veins.

Stella has her secrets—ones I wish I could stay to uncover. Without a chance to reconsider, I heft her into my arms. Her warm body curls against my chest, her hand twisting into my fur trustingly. My heart pounds harder as I walk her over to her bed. I settle her atop the sheets and gently pull the quilt over her.

The scent of her clings to my fur and drives me wild.

Sleepy blue eyes blink open at me. We merely stare at each other for a moment, and I take the chance to commit every detail of her to memory.

"Are you leaving?" she asks, voice thick with sleep.

I nod, not trusting my voice.

A look of sadness dances in her eyes as she begins to rise.

"I need to get you some medicine before you go."

Shaking my head, I pull back the binding on my chest and show her the healed skin.

"Oh," she says. "That's handy."

We stare at each other, the air around us becoming thicker. A part of me senses she doesn't want me to leave. That same voice urges me to stay, but I cannot. I have responsibilities to attend to. Once the matters at home are settled, perhaps I can return and—

I shake my head and straighten my spine.

"Thank you," I whisper. "I'll never forget you, Stella."

Tears dance at the corners of her eyes before she quickly

blinks them away. My heart threatens to shatter in my chest. I want to take her into my arms and soothe her. Curling my claws into my palms, the prick of pain stops me.

"Be safe out there," she whispers.

Refusing to succumb to my weakness, I turn from her and head towards the door.

"Goodbye, Ciaryn." Her soft voice tickles my ear. I nearly groan at how perfect my name sounds coming from her lips.

My claws lock around the doorknob, and I yank it open. Early morning birds sing from above, but *The Woods* are still quiet. My body screams at me to stay, but I don't listen.

"Goodbye, Stella," I say before launching onto all fours and sprinting towards the rising sun.

5

______

STELLA

The tavern is solemn tonight.

It matches my mood. The few patrons lingering at the bar barely speak to each other. It's been quiet all evening. Word had spread about the missing wolfman, and many had decided to stay in rather than risk their chances with him on the loose.

If only I could tell them he is far from this town.

It is ridiculous to be sad over Ciaryn. I barely knew him for more than a few hours, yet part of me hoped he would change his mind and return. However, when I woke up hours later, and he hadn't come back, I knew I'd never see the wolfman again. As the sun set, I had made peace with it.

Despite my selfish wants, it is best he left when he did.

When I arrived this evening, Old Bill had told me the news and how desperate the hunters—especially Timson—were to find him. My stomach sinks at the thought of what he had planned for Ciaryn. The mounted heads of animals on the tavern's wall make my skin crawl. The idea that Ciaryn's was meant to join them nearly makes me lose the contents of my stomach.

As the final two patrons pay for their ale and slip out into the night, Old Bill emerges from the backroom.

"Why don't you go ahead and head home, Stella? I don't think anyone else is coming tonight. You shouldn't be out late with that creature on the loose."

"Are you sure?" I ask, wiping up spilled ale on the counter. "I don't mind staying."

Old Bill nods.

"I'm sure. I'll lock up after you leave."

Usually, I'd love the chance to leave early, but I know an empty cottage awaits me. Again, my thoughts travel to the wolf-man. Perhaps I have just been on my own for too long, and his brief companionship had given me the connection I've longed for. He was grumpy and growly, but I had liked that about him. Ciaryn made me feel safe and intrigued me in ways no human man ever has.

As I collect my cloak from the hook and slip into the cold night air, I wonder where he is. As I journey back to my cottage, I can't help but hope he's there waiting for me. The fantasy plays out. One in which he's waiting for me at my small kitchen table saying he's changed his mind, and well—I don't know exactly what will come after that. The thought of never seeing him again tears at my heart. How can you miss someone you barely know?

My despair only worsens as my small cottage comes into view. I should've lit a candle before leaving so it's not dark inside. The last bits of sunset have already bled from the sky, and *The Woods* look particularly ominous this evening.

Finding the key in my pocket, I put it in the door and turn the lock.

There is a soft rustling at my back, followed by a deep growl. My blood runs cold, and I slowly turn. My knees nearly buckle as I take in the formidable figures standing there.

Timson is at the front with a large hunting rifle strapped at his back. At his back are five other armed hunters and two vicious dogs, restrained by leather leashes. Foaming saliva pours from the corners of their snarling mouths.

My hand flies to my chest.

"Oh, Timson, you scared me," I say, leaning back against the door.

He drinks from his flask before discarding it. Red rims his beady eyes, and sweat collects along his brow.

"Sorry about that." His words are slightly slurred. "You shouldn't be out this late with a beast on the loose."

I swallow before shrugging.

"Old Bill needed me so..."

I let the sentence trail off as Timson approaches. His gait eats up the distance between us, and his hunters follow closely behind. My blood freezes in my veins. I need to get inside and lock the door. This situation is dangerous. This far away from the village, no one can hear me—not that they would be much help against him anyway.

I clear my throat.

"Have you had any luck finding the wolfman?" I ask, hoping he'll remember his task and leave me alone.

Timson gives a dismissive shake of his head.

"We've been searching *The Woods* all day. The neighboring villages as well. The creature's scent seems to have disappeared altogether." His bleary eyes narrow at me. "Yet, my dogs keep circling your cottage. Why is that?"

My mouth runs dry.

"I—um, well, living this close to *The Woods*, it wouldn't be far a stretch to assume he passed by here while fleeing."

Timson takes another step closer to me, his body nearly brushing mine.

"Have you seen the demon?" he demands—his breath reeks of whiskey.

"No."

He inhales deeply, something kindling in his gaze. A lazy smile spreads over her lips as bile races up my throat. I remember his drunken declarations last night at the old mill. The blood in my veins ices over.

"You know, Stella, you shouldn't live this remote." He leans closer to my face, and my back flattens against the door. "But it does have its perks. Lots of privacy."

I nod, not knowing what else to say. His hand falls beside my head against the door. His stench nearly makes my eyes water.

"Have you given my offer any more thought?"

I swallow, fumbling behind me to find the doorknob. My hand wraps around it, and I twist it, preparing to slip through.

"Look, Timson, it's late—I'm tired—and I should get inside with a wolfman on the loose. We will talk more tomorrow at the tavern."

I push the door open and slip inside without waiting for his reply. Before I can shut it, Timson's hand wraps around the edge of the door. With more strength than I thought he had, he forces the door open and follows me in. Panic sends a shiver down my spine.

"What are you—"

"How about I don't give you a choice, Stella? No one is here but my men." He stomps towards me, and I stumble back towards the kitchen table. "You've been disrespecting me for far too long."

"You need to leave—you're drunk and—"

He presses closer to me, the front of our bodies flush. The corner of the kitchen table presses into my spine. The pungent taste of fear coats my tongue, especially as I feel the hardness in his trousers pressing into me.

My hands reach behind me, searching for anything sharp. Timson takes his opportunity and grasps my upper arms, leaning me slightly backward.

"Stop, Timson! I'll scream—I'll—"

"My men will not save you—they'll want a turn once I'm done." His yellow teeth are on full display as he smiles down at me. "This has been long overdue."

I scream and thrash in his hold. Kicking at his shin with my boated feet, Timson dodges my assault and holds me tighter. His hands find the high neck of my gown, and I nearly vomit at the feel of his fingers on my naked skin. I try to twist away, knowing what he intends to do next. I bump against the table, and it rattles as its contents shift.

Timson freezes as he peers over my shoulder. Wrapping a hand around my throat, his grip holds firm as I claw at him. He keeps me pinned as he reaches for a piece of cloth. Unraveling the bloody fabric, I watch as a single silver bullet hits the table with a light thud. I hadn't bothered cleaning up from last night.

As I watch the realization dawn on Timson's face, the air shifts and my situation goes from bad to worse. His dark eyes frost over.

"You fucking bitch. It was here!" His hand around my throat tightens. My fingernails shred his skin, but his grip never loosens. "I'm going to kill you. You hear me? Kill you!"

His other hand wraps around my throat as well, and my breathing becomes entirely restricted. I fight to stay awake and to keep fighting. Darkness dances around the edges of my vision. The deadly look in Timson's eyes tells me there is no stopping him.

I cannot believe this is how my story ends. I escaped certain death only to find it at the hands of another man. There are so many things I should've done to avoid this, but it's pointless to dwell on them now. I have moments left before I'm gone. Perhaps it is the lack of air, but my heart reaches towards Ciaryn. If only he had stayed. If only—

A low growl cuts through the air—deeper than the sounds from the hunting dogs. At first, I think I've imagined it, but

Timson releases his hold, and I suck down precious lungfuls of air. He whirls around towards my open door and slings the gun off his back.

"On second thought," he snarls, gripping my arm and pulling me out towards the front of the cottage. "I'm going to make you watch me slaughter that beast."

Dragging me out of my house with force, he tosses me onto the damp grass of the front lawn. My head still feels cloudy as I try to gulp down more air. Timson marches towards the other hunters, and they each grip their guns.

"Spread out and find that fucking beast!" Timson commands, training his gun toward *The Woods*.

The hunting dogs are let off their leashes. They snap and snarl towards the treeline. A deep growl permeates the air just as they disappear into the darkness. Rushed footsteps charge back toward us, and the two hunting dogs whimper as they run in the opposite direction, tails tucked firmly between their legs. A few hunters shout at them, but they are long gone.

"You!" snarls Timson. "Get closer."

One of the hunters—whose name I never bothered to learn—swallows before training his gun on the forest's edge. He ambles over, his boots dragging along the damp grass. *The Woods* seem impossibly large as he reaches the first row of trees. After a couple more steps, he pauses, lowering his gun and turning back towards us.

"There's nothing—" The words break off on a wet gurgle as blood spills from his mouth.

The hunter looks down in time to see a clawed hand emerge from his chest with his heart clasped in its palm. Pulling back, his body drops like a doll's in a clatter of twisted limbs. Above him stands Ciaryn, his eyes like two golden fires. His ruby lips pull back in a snarl. He tosses the organ towards the other hunters, and it lands with a wet slap.

My heart thunders in my chest at the sight of him. He's returned to me. He's—

"Shoot it!" Timson yells.

The sound of bullets raining echoes around me. Screaming, I cover my ears and drop further onto the wet grass. It is hard to see in the darkness. My eyes wildly search for Ciaryn—needing to know he is okay. There is a streak of movement from the corner of my eye. I barely register it before a hunter is snatched off their feet with a loud yell. The others turn towards the noise only for a few moments later, another to be grabbed.

The sounds of firing guns grow quiet as Timson becomes the only one left. He yells as he goes to reload his weapon—his trembling hands cause silver bullets to fall to the grass. A soft whooshing sound echoes through the air, quickly followed by another and then another. Three round objects roll toward Timson, and he freezes.

There at his feet are the severed heads of the rest of his hunting party. I can't help but whimper at the brutal sight. Timson whirls on me. I scramble away as he stomps towards me, but he's too quick. Brandishing a knife, he hauls me up against his chest and presses the blade to my throat.

From the treeline, Ciaryn emerges, prowling on all fours as blood drips from his mouth. I whimper as Timson presses the blade harder against me. My hands wrap around his arm, but he is stronger than I am.

"I'll kill her, beast. Just let me go, or I'll slit her throat."

Ciaryn's eyes narrow. They connect with mine, and I will him not to act rashly. Timson has lost it, and I know one wrong move with the knife will mean my death. The blade presses harder against me, and I'm surprised he hasn't broken skin.

Ciaryn whines before turning and disappearing into the darkness. Timson pushes me to the ground and reaches for his discarded gun. He fires rapidly in Ciaryn's direction.

"No!" I scream.

Timson doesn't stop; he just keeps firing and firing. A flash of movement dances at the corner of my eyes. I turn in time to see Ciaryn emerge from behind my cottage. I have no idea how he moved so quickly, but I don't get long to consider it. Not as Ciaryn launches, claws extended, and locks his jaws around Timson's neck with a satisfying snap. The man screams, dropping his gun as scarlet pours down his body and soaks his clothes.

Ciaryn locks his claws around his arms and twists Timson to look up at him.

"Die, human," he snarls into his face. "For touching her against her will, for daring to hurt her—you will understand the meaning of pain."

There is a wet snap sound as Ciaryn embeds his claws in Timson's arms. The hunter screams and soaks the front of his trousers. He thrashes and yells, but it is of no use. With one mighty tug, Timson's arms are ripped from his body and tossed onto the overgrown grass. Blood pours from his shoulders and soaks the ground. His mouth is parted, but no sound comes out. The hunter's body twitches slightly before going completely still.

The night air is quiet as death surrounds my cottage. My fingers sink into the wet grass as I take in the gruesome sight. Such violence should repulse me—scare me—but when Ciaryn's eyes meet mine, it takes all my restraint not to throw myself into his arms.

His approach is tentative as if expecting me to recoil from him. I merely reach for him, allowing the hands that have just slaughtered so many to help me to my feet. His pine scent calms me and sets my blood on fire.

"You saved me," I whisper, staring up at him. "How'd you get here so fast? I thought you'd—"

"Left?" he interrupts. "I tried to—ran for hours before turning back. I had to see you again."

"Why?"

"I don't know."

My hand slowly reaches up and cups his cheek. His soft fur slips between my fingers.

"Well, I'm glad you came back. Are you hurt?"

Ciaryn shakes his head. "Are you?"

"No, Timson, he—well—you stopped him before anything could happen."

A low growl slips from his lips as his hands reach for my waist. Their warm weight soothes my fragile nerves.

"I'll always protect you. It's the least I could do after—"

I wrinkle my nose. "You don't have to repay my healing with personal protection."

"It's not repayment, Stella. I want to keep you safe— need to."

The heat in his gaze burns me alive. Warmth spreads along my cheeks. Even though being in his arms is wonderful, I can't help but focus on the carnage littering my front lawn.

"I'll have to move. I'm sure people will come looking for them." Taking his hand, I lead him towards the door. "We should get inside. More could already be on their way."

Ciaryn's hand tightens in mine.

"I won't leave you to deal with this mess alone."

I nod, my eyes snagging at the dried blood on his mouth.

"Come," I say. "Let me clean you off."

Just like the previous night, he settles onto my small wooden chair. After locking the door, I find a clean rag, wet it, and clean off the blood along his mouth and hands. Moving to his chest, I'm happy to see his wounds fully healed. Once I'm satisfied he's clean, I drop the rag onto the kitchen table. My eyes take in the previous night's mess, and everything hits me at once.

Oh *gods*, how terrible tonight could've gone if Ciaryn hadn't shown up. If Timson hadn't been stopped, he would've—I would've—tears pool in my eyes and fall down my cheeks. My strength leaves me as the fear from this evening washes over me. Before I can clatter to the floor, Ciaryn is there. He catches me against his chest, and I curl against him.

With steady strides, he walks us towards the side of my bed. His warmth leaves me only momentarily as he kneels before me and unlaces my boots. My numb fingers find the lacings of my dress and undo them. Tossing the heavy gown over my head, Ciaryn rids me of my socks. In a daze, I fall against the soft sheets.

Gathering the quilt in his hands, he gently pulls it over me.

"Sleep, Stella. I'll keep watch from the floor."

Before he can turn away, my hand snags his wrist. I don't want to be alone in this bed. Not after tonight—not ever. Ciaryn makes me feel safe. His scent and warmth are a comfort —one I desperately need right now.

"Stay," I whisper, tugging him towards me. "Please."

Ciaryn looks conflicted for a moment. I tug at his hand again, and he pulls back the sheets. I slide back to give him room. His pine scent invades my lungs. The evening chill is remedied when his warmth seeps into my side.

I've never been so forward in my life, but I can't bring myself to care. My arms wrap around his strong middle, and I snuggle deeper against his soft fur. His claws skim up and down my back, as he growls softly. The sound soothes me almost as much as his presence.

Like last night, I feel safe—even more so now that I am in his arms. The horrors of this evening finally leave my mind. Something unfurls in my chest—permanent and all-consuming. A fresh wave of warmth spreads throughout my body. Pressing my cheek to his chest, I let the rhythmic sound of his heartbeat lull me to sleep.

6

___

CIARYN

Being this close to Stella is beautiful torture.

All night, my body was painfully aware of her closeness. Her supple curves pressed softly against the muscles of my side. Her smooth thigh rested atop my legs. Stella's lovely face is relaxed in sleep and close enough for me to count each freckle decorating her nose and cheeks—all one-hundred-and-thirty-seven.

Warm sunlight streams into the room. A slash of gold falls across her eyes, and Stella sighs, twisting her small hands into my fur. I swallow my groan and dig my claws into the sheets. My body is taut with restraint, but the soft sigh that leaves her full lips nearly snaps it.

Despite the desire pumping through my veins, the night had been quiet. With the rising sun illuminating her small cottage, I realize leaving Stella behind is no longer an option. It isn't only my selfish desires that demand that she remain at my side, but also because her safety is my paramount concern. Bodies and blood litter her front yard. There will be more hunters once the news spreads of the ones who have gone missing.

I refuse to bring trouble to Stella's door.

Now the question is, where will we go? I could take her back to the den. She would be safe there—protected by my pack. That is if I still have a pack. Though she would have to be...

Stella stirs against my side again. A content sight leaves her mouth, and the leg atop mine lifts higher, hooking over my hip. A growl vibrates my chest. I'm awash in her sweet, floral scent —greedily breathing it into my lungs. It would take nothing for my claws to tear her thin shift into ribbons. With a gentle push, she'd be on her back, staring up at me as I sank my knot deep inside of her—binding her to me permanently.

I shake myself and grind my teeth together. I'm a bastard for thinking such things, especially given what she went through last night. Stella deserves to be courted and treated with kindness, not rutted upon by a wild animal like myself. If I wish to keep her, I must consider her humanity and delicateness more.

It's also plausible that she doesn't desire me in that way. To her, I am nothing more than a protector. It would be painful to go through life, never feeling her soft body beneath mine, but I would do it. I am not saying that I would leave her in peace. No, I fear that from this point on, Stella is either by my side, or I will spend the rest of my eternal life haunting her from the shadows, following wherever she goes.

That is why I must choose my next move carefully. If I take her to the den, she can never leave. The only humans allowed inside are mates. My mother was the last human to reside there. Her passing was not only a death blow to my father but plunged our pack into a dark era. When she died, so did the mating bonds that were meant to grow inside all of us. No one has found their mate in the years since she's been gone.

As a pup, I dreamed about finding mine, but that desire withered with age. Gazing down at Stella, I realize this is the pull my father felt all those years ago. This instant desire—this need to protect her and keep her—is all-consuming. I know she is mine. Now, I just have to prove that I deserve her.

What will be her reaction when I tell her of my longing? I take some solstice in the way she clings to me in sleep. Stella is not repulsed by me. Her body shifts closer, and my cock grows even harder. All the blood in my body races towards it, hardening the knot at its base and begging me to sink it deep into her wet heat.

Swallowing my snarl, I carefully reach down and adjust myself, willing my errant cock to behave.

My movements were not as subtle as I had hoped as Stella's leg tightens around me—a soft moan blooms from between her lips. Sleepy blue eyes blink open as her mouth pulls into a grin. Color swims on her freckled cheeks as she realizes just how close our bodies are.

To my delight, she doesn't try to move away—only loosens her grip on the fur along my chest.

"Good morning," she says, her voice rough. "You're really warm. Deliciously so."

I'm too distracted by her beauty to stifle my groan. It lands between us as my hand wanders to her hip. Stella shivers at the touch, and I gently squeeze her side. Dragging her closer, I am rewarded by her soft gasp and a fresh wave of her scent. This time, it is spicier—headier.

Her blue eyes dip to my mouth.

"Can a wolfman kiss a human?"

Stella's question is barely above a whisper, yet it steals all the breath from my lungs. Surely, I am dreaming. How could someone as beautiful and perfect as Stella offer me this chance to taste her? My head spins, and my cock strains against the front of my pants.

"Yes." My voice sounds strange to my own ears.

"Do you want to kiss me?"

My whole body shudders as I grapple with the last tendrils

of my self-control. I have to be sure she wants this. I could not bear it if Stella came to regret anything between us.

"More than anything." My hand on her hip tightens. "But only if you want me to. After last night..."

I trail off, and Stella's eyes widen. Coming fully awake, she throws back the quilt and begins to rise. I want to curse myself for being a fool. She was offering me a taste, and now she is turning away.

However, instead of sliding out of bed, Stella surprises me again by putting her hands on my shoulders and pushing me onto my back. In one fluid movement, her body settles atop mine. Her ample breasts tease the neckline of her shift. The creamy swells of each one make my mouth water. Lithe thighs settle on either side of my hips.

The golden sunlight washes her in color, making her glow like a goddess.

"For years, I allowed Timson to dictate how I felt about my body. I'd dress in ways to keep his hands from finding my bare skin. I feared desire—sex—knowing that he was watching me. I couldn't truly be myself and explore what I wanted because a part of me was terrified he'd be the one I was forced to be with." She smiles as I growl at her mistreatment. "You freed me from him, and I am grateful."

My hands fall to her hips again—claws digging into her soft flesh.

"I only wish our paths had crossed sooner. I could've saved you from years of his torment." I swallow. "But you do not have to kiss me out of gratitude, Stella."

Her smile broadens. Wickedness tips the edges of her lips.

"I'm not," she sighs. "I want to because you gave me something more than my freedom."

"What?"

Biting her bottom lip, Stella leans down her body, becoming flush with my own. Her warmth seeps into me. Each of her soft curves presses into my hard edges, and all thoughts empty from my head.

"Desire," she whispers against my lips.

Stella kisses me, and my life is forever changed.

The soft brush of her lips makes and unmakes me. Before, I was Ciaryn—a wolf on the run from his responsibility. Now I am Ciaryn—protector of Stella, the worshipper of the goddess in my arms. Her lips are an addiction, and the tentative touch soon gives way to something more animalistic.

Her hands tangle into my fur as her lips part. In an instant, my tongue slides into her mouth and gently glides along hers. She doesn't fight me for dominance. Instead, she lovingly caresses mine—teasing it with gentle touches. My blood heats into an inferno. She tastes of honey, and I want to drink her down.

My claws skim up her back, and she moans, writhing against me. She's up high enough on my chest that the supple swells of her ass brush my stiff cock. If she notices my painfully aroused state, she doesn't mention it. I can scent her arousal and say a prayer that I'll be able to taste her nectar directly from the source.

Pulling back, her eyes are wild as she gazes down at me. Her chest rises and falls with ragged breaths. The sleeve of her shift hangs from her shoulder, exposing an expanse of pale gold skin. My nose nuzzles against her neck before licking and nipping my way along her throat. My canines elongate and encourage me to mark her as mine, but I hold off. I'm being too greedy—she's already given me more than enough by allowing my kisses.

My mouth continues down her neck and over her shoulder. I lick lower, tasting the smooth skin of her collarbone. Soft mewls of pleasure slip from her lips. She rocks atop my body as if desperate for more. My lips find the top of her shift and gently prod the soft fabric, painfully aware of how close her breasts are.

"Take it off."

Her soft command surprises me enough to raise my eyes and look at her. Clear blue eyes shine down at me, and color swims in her cheeks, making her even more beautiful.

"Take it off," she repeats, cupping my hands around her shift. "I don't want any barriers between us."

In an instant, it is nothing but tatters, my claws making quick work of the fabric. Stella giggles at my haste, and I quickly toss the ruined garment to the side. The breath stills in my lungs as I take her in. Sitting back ever so slightly, the sunlight caresses her body. Perk breasts tipped with hard, pink nipples make my mouth water. Her waist gives into lush hips and thighs. Nestled between them is a patch of dark golden hair. I can feel her arousal soaking my chest. The smell of her is intoxicating.

Freckles cover her shoulders and chest, and I'll be sure to count all of them one day soon.

My claw reaches up to cup one of her breasts. She moans as my tongue darts out to taste her fully. I work the tight bud as I roughly shape her other breast in my hand. I alternate between the two, greedy to savor as much of her as possible. Her hips writhe, and moans of pleasure pour from her mouth.

"I've never been with a human before." My confession is snarled against her breast.

Blue eyes peer down at me.

"I've never been with a wolfman."

Something snaps inside me, my grip on her tightening.

"I'll ruin you for all other men," I vow against her breast. "You'll never crave one of your human lovers again."

A fresh blush spreads across her cheeks as she meets my eyes.

"I've never had one of those either."

All of my hard-won restraint snaps in an instant.

"Tell me what you want," I command.

"You."

I shiver with delight.

"What do you want me to do to you?"

"Everything."

I meet her heated stare as my claws skim down her front. Gliding along her smooth skin, my fingers find that small patch of hair and gently part her. I hiss at how soaked she is—her warm, wet softness presses against my palm as I cup her. Stella gasps, and her hands fall to my legs for support.

"Do you want me to make you come?" I ask. "Will you let me taste your sweet pussy?"

Her mouth opens and closes as I continue to stroke between her thighs. Slowly, my claw finds her back entrance's tight ring of muscle. Her eyes fly open as I gently prod it.

"Will you let me claim this hole one day too?"

Stella grinds against me, riding my arm for all she's worth. My little human is desperate for any ounce of friction.

"Ciaryn," she cries. "Please, I need you."

My name on her lips moves me. In a flash, my hands snag her around the waist and yank her up the bed. Her hands fall to the headboard as I position her dripping cunt above my face. It is so pretty and pink. I take a moment to marvel at its beauty before pressing a loving kiss to it. Stella's body grows taut as I lick her clit with the broad side of my tongue. The little bundle of nerves causes her hips to canter with each stroke.

"Ciaryn! Oh, I've never—"

"This pussy is too delicious. I'd kill a thousand men just for one lick of your perfect cunt."

"Yes!" she hisses, her knuckles going white atop the headboard.

I slip my tongue into her opening and taste her fully. The musky, sweet flavor of her arousal slips over my tongue. She is indecently wet. To know I did this to her is a particular delight. Her hips grind against my face, causing my tongue to go deeper. I twist it, mimicking the same motion my cock will once I'm able to be inside her. The knowledge that I'm the only one who's had her like this encourages the primal part of me to claim her.

I must be patient even as words of praise spill from her mouth.

"I like how powerful you are," she moans. "I like knowing you spilled blood for me."

"I'd do it a hundred times," I snarl, sucking her clit into my mouth.

Her body goes tight. Slipping a finger into her entrance, her pussy greedily clamps down on the intrusion. The tightness of her core makes my head spin. Gently, I fuck her with my finger, hooking it in a way that has the breath shuddering out of her.

"Does that make me a bad person?" she asks.

My hand lifts from her hip to gently swat the fleshy mound of her ass. Stella gasps, and her eyes fly open.

"It just means you know who you belong to. That you are meant to be mine."

Slipping a second finger into her, my lips wrap around her clit, and Stella is done for. She comes all over my face, soaking me in a rush of her sweetness. Her delicate inner muscles tighten on my thrusting fingers as she shakes through her plea-sure. My name spills from her lips as her muscles lose their rigidity.

I don't give her a moment's reprieve.

Pulling my fingers from her, I gently cup her hips and toss her face down towards the end of the bed. Her arms are weak, but she manages to keep herself up on all fours. My cock bobs as I shift behind her. Gripping her round ass cheeks, I lower my face to her heated center once more. It glistens with her arousal. She shudders at the first press of my tongue.

"Do you know what it means when a wolfman claims a human?" I ask.

Stella shakes her head. Her hands grip the sheets to keep her upright. My tongue nudges her untouched hole, and she screams. I do it again, delighted when her hips push back against me.

"A wolfman mates for life. When he finds his human mate, he claims her with his knot—filling her with his seed until she grows round with his children." My tongue dips into her back entrance again. "Once she has been claimed, they will be one. Forever."

My fingers spear into her greedy cunt. The quickening of her pussy tells me she's already close to another climax.

"Tell me you want that, Stella. I need to hear you say it."

My fingers scissor her just right, and her back bows.

"Yes. Yes! I want that—I want you!"

Her screamed confession erupts in my veins. Without warning, I spear my tongue into her asshole and push deep. My fingers fuck her faster and faster until she erupts on the bed. Her arousal soaks my hand, but my movements never stop. She shakes through her climax.

Snaking my tongue out of her ass, I lick her clean between her thighs. She is panting and twitching by the time I'm down. Red engulfs her cheeks and chest as I wrap her shaking body in my arms. Her eyes are open, but I'm not sure she's aware of anything. I settle her against me, letting the rapid beating of her heart soothe me.

Stella wants this—she wants us. She is mine, and I will have her fully once I am sure she is somewhere safe.

After a few moments of silence, Stella blinks and curls into my side. Biting her lip, her hands skim down my front. I swallow as they reach dangerously close to my hard cock. Without thinking, I wrap my hand around her wrist to stop her.

"Don't you want me to—you know?"

I kiss her soundly, sharing her taste with her.

"In time. All I want now is to take care of you and ensure you're safe."

As much as the primal urge to have her burns in my blood, I have to get her somewhere secure first. She wants me—now I need to protect my mate at all costs and never give her a reason to regret her life with me. My animalistic need to bite and fuck her full of my seed can wait. Tucking her naked body against me, I relish the feeling of her soft skin.

Stella smiles up at her, saying nothing and everything all at once. The intimacy flows freely between us, and I feel like the luckiest male in the world to have found her. Her carnal nature is evident; I can't wait to explore it fully. I can tell Stella feels the same from the gleam in her eyes.

"So," she says, nuzzling my chest, "when do we leave?"

7

STELLA

Standing in front of my cottage, sadness ripples through me.

I'll miss my quiet home. It was the first place I could truly call mine. I have loved my time in Moon's Hallow. Working at the tavern with Old Bill and spending lazy afternoons curled up on my couch reading as the sun filtered through the windows brought me comfort. The memories I have here will be tucked away into my heart forever.

Now, as I feel Ciaryn's soft fur brush against my bare arm, I'm ready to start a new adventure.

Everything I wanted to bring is tucked inside the small leather satchel draped across my body: a few thin dresses, a couple of books, and a smattering of herbs for treating wounds and illnesses.

With Timson dead, I feel free. The dress I'm wearing is a testament to that.

Additionally, I love the way Ciaryn stares at the bare skin of my arms and chest like he wants to devour me whole—he nearly did this morning. The heady memories come rushing back, bringing a fresh flush to my cheeks. Ciaryn has a wicked, *wicked* mouth. Part of the thrill had been his animalistic nature —something that delights me in ways I didn't think possible.

Ciaryn expertly attended to my pleasure. His care for me, priority of my needs, and protection of me have made my newfound feelings grow for him quickly.

How is it that I've known him barely a day and feel like he has been a part of my life forever? Perhaps it has to do with what he called us—mates. He demanded my assurances that he was what I wanted, and I meant every word. I never want to be parted from him. It is a sudden realization, but I mean it all the same.

I've never felt the way I do about Ciaryn for anyone.

That's why I have no regrets as I turn away from my cottage and climb atop his back. I know he will keep me safe. I thought I wanted freedom—to belong to no one but myself. Now I see how wrong I was. I'm ready to bind myself to him and enjoy our shared future.

The feel of his fur on my inner thighs brings back memories of our delicious morning. His lewd words had caused me to blush. More out of excitement than embarrassment. My pussy heats, wanting to feel his mouth and fingers on me again. Ciaryn scents the air, and I feel a low growl permeate his chest. Shifting back and forth, I wrap my arms around his neck and hold tight.

"Ready?" he asks.

I nod, tightening my hold.

Without another word, Ciaryn springs forward and into *The Woods*. I don't look back—I don't do anything but rest my cheek against Ciaryn's strong back. I'm sure some would say I'm being foolish and acting rashly. However, I've trusted my heart before, and it guided me out from under my father's thumb. Now it's telling me to go with Ciaryn wherever that may take us.

The dark forest swallows us up. Towering green trees and unruly branches pass us in a blur. Ciaryn navigates the uneven terrain gracefully. The fresh scent of grass tickles my nose. I inhale the spicy pine scent of my wolfman and let it soothe me. I listen to the strong pounding of his heart—the rhythm matching my own—as we travel toward our future.

Together.

I HAVE no idea how long we travel for.

Truth be told, I dozed off a few times on our journey, only to jolt awake when I felt my grip on Ciaryn slipping. I came fully awake as he slowed down near a roaring stream. We are still deep in *The Woods*. The stories of its danger and bloodthirsty inhabitants mean little to me with Ciaryn by my side.

The setting sun spills through the branches of the surrounding trees, casting the area around us in harsh shadows.

Ciaryn finally stops at the base of one of the trees. I slip from his back, my muscles sore from holding on tightly. Stretching my arms over my head, Ciaryn rises to his full height and does the same. The depth of his strength steals my breath. His golden eyes sparkle down at me.

"We'll rest here for the night," he declares. "I've put a good distance between us and the village."

His finger curls around a strand of my hair that's come loose from my braid.

"I'll find something for us to eat. The stream should be warm enough if you want to wash up."

I sigh.

"That sounds wonderful."

Digging into my small bag, I fetch a bar of lavender soap. Unbraiding my hair, I take the leather tie and secure my tresses into a messy bun at the top of my head. Turning towards the roaring stream, I kick off my shoes and unlace the back of my gown. Letting it and my shift pool at my feet, I scoop them up and hang them from a low branch of a nearby tree.

A low howl cuts through the clearing and goosebumps break out along my flesh. Turning to look over my bare shoulder, my eyes connect with Ciaryn's. The noticeable bulge in his pants makes my mouth water. I look at it pointedly and raise a brow.

"Do you want to join me?" I ask, skimming my hand down my naked sides.

Ciaryn growls again before shaking his head.

"Must feed you," he rasps, his voice deeper than before.

A smile curls my lips. "Suit yourself."

Walking into the stream, a soft moan slips from my lips. The water is a perfect temperature and laps against my bare skin. My nipples harden instantly. I walk deeper into the water until it reaches my shoulders—the soft bottom of the stream squishes between my toes. The rushing water soothes my muscles.

Ciaryn disappears briefly before reappearing with a few dead rabbits. My stomach rolls partly from hunger but mainly from the sight. I'll tell him I prefer a more plant-based diet when we are more settled. He makes quick work of skinning them and setting up a fire near the edge of the stream. His eyes return to me once the meat rests over the flames to cook.

I smile, reaching for the soap to begin lathering my body. Ciaryn's hungry gaze tracks every movement, and I shiver under the intensity.

"So," I say. "How much longer until we make it to our destination?"

It takes a moment for him to register I've asked him a question. Shaking his head, he prowls closer to the edge of the stream.

"Not much longer. We could've made it there tonight, but I wanted you to rest."

The soap foams in my hands. I use the suds to clean under my arms and along my neck. The lavender scent surrounds me as I scrub away the day's dirt.

"Do more of your people live there? Your pack?" I ask.

Ciaryn makes a low noise before nodding once. I float the bar of soap towards him as he washes the blood off his hands from the rabbits. His eyes devour me as I walk closer to the stream's edge. The water is lower over here, barely covering my breasts.

"You don't like talking about them," I whisper. "Or where you're from."

Ciaryn's eyes shudder as he lowers his head.

"It's complicated. I left when they needed me most."

My hand snakes out from the water to wrap around his. With a gentle squeeze, I guide his gaze back to mine.

"Tell me."

Ciaryn stares at me for a moment. The silence stretches until I'm nearly certain he won't continue. Then, I feel his hand tighten on mine before he moves quickly, pulling my soaking body from the water and rubbing me against him. I gasp at the sensation.

"What are you doing?" I giggle.

The evening air is cool against my damp skin, and Ciaryn is so warm I can't help but wrap my arms around his neck and hold him closer.

"Getting you dry," he replies, running his arms down my sides.

"Hmm," I sigh. "How chivalrous. I'm sure this has nothing to do with the fact that I'm naked and dripping wet."

Ciaryn chuckles, nuzzling into my neck. Despite how good

he feels, I can't get swept up in him just yet. I need some answers first.

"Tell me where we are going, Ciaryn."

My wolfman sighs and then presses a kiss to my cheek. He tucks me into his arms and holds me so we are at eye level with each other. *The Woods* are quiet tonight. Whatever danger lurks here knows better than to venture too close to us.

After a moment of silence, Ciaryn nods.

"My pack's den. It's the safest place for you," he says. "It's a large cavern with plenty of tunnels and natural springs. Inside, dozens of dwellings are carved into the rock for each pack member to house themselves and their families."

"Does your family live there?" I ask softly, wanting to know more about him.

Ciaryn's golden eyes dim.

"For a time," he says. "My mother was human—as all our mates are—and she lived happily with my father for many years. When I was still young, hunters found her with me. They didn't take one of their own being claimed by a beast too well. By the time my father heard her screams and came for us, it was too late. He was never the same after that."

All the air leaves my lungs as I picture the horrible scene. Ciaryn—young and afraid—as his mother is slain before his eyes. What an awful thing to behold.

His claws skim along my back as he clears the roughness from his voice.

"My father tried to be a good male—a good alpha to our pack—but he's been slowly dying these last thirty years." Ciaryn swallows. "And when he passed a week ago, I could tell he was finally happy—knowing he would soon be with my mother again."

My heart aches as I cup his soft cheek. Pressing a gentle kiss to his forehead, I nestle deeper into his embrace.

"I'm so sorry, Ciaryn."

He shakes his head.

"I'm a coward, Stella. When he died, I—I didn't know what to do. I was supposed to be his successor and lead our pack after his passing, but I couldn't. My grief made me flee, and now I don't know how they'll react to my return."

"We'll face it together," I breathe. "Tell them all you've told me, and they'll understand."

I drag his eyes back up to mine when he still looks uncertain.

"A good leader is not cruel and unfeeling. Believe me, I would know."

Dark memories flood me. Long-buried fragments of my previous life threaten to shred the beautiful future I've found for myself. My father was evil—as was my brother—and had I not fled when I did, I would've become their prisoner one way or another. I never would've met Ciaryn. The thought makes me hold on to him tighter.

His golden eyes search mine, and his ears flatten. I know he has questions for me about my past. I'll give him answers soon enough. Right now, all I want is to feel his arms around me. That is why I merely smile and rub my nose along his.

"My tale is also a sad one. The family I was born into was not a kind one."

Ciaryn's eyes flash.

"Whatever secrets lurk in your past, Stella, I'll protect you from them. You'll always be safe with me."

My lips pull into a grin.

"I believe you," I say before giggling softly. "I've only known you a short time, and yet, this feels so permanent—as if we were always meant to be together."

"We are," Ciaryn growls.

I nod my head, heat flaring within my body. With him so close, I feel safe and whole. The demons of my past are far away from here. I believe Ciaryn when he says he'll protect me. I feel secure enough to do things I never have before.

"It should be ridiculous—desiring you like I do." My teeth sink into my lower lip as I look up at him. "Well, I suppose it's no more ridiculous than wanting to put a wolfman's cock in my mouth."

Ciaryn's sharp inhale is music to my ears. His claws dig into the skin of my back, making me sigh. Fire burns in his golden gaze.

"Stella." His snarl of my name breaks off on a groan as my hand drifts down his body. He shudders as I palm his aching length through his trousers. "Are you sure? You do not have—"

"I want to," I say. "More than anything."

I rub my hand along his hardness. The length of him causes me to turn slippery between my thighs. With my other hand, I push on his shoulder and urge him onto his back. Ciaryn's hands fall to my waist, and I know he'll want to place me atop his face, but I won't allow that yet. Wiggling away from his hands, I shuffle down his legs and fall between his spread thighs.

"This is all for you, Ciaryn," I sigh. "I want to please you."

Together, we work in tandem to shed his pants. What greets my eyes steals my breath. His impressive length rises proudly between his legs. The dark flesh of his cock gives way to a round head already leaking a milky bead of seed. Dark veins decorate the side. There is a circular ridge around the base of his cock, growing in size by the second.

I have no idea how he'll fit inside of me, but my body is more than willing to try.

Taking him into my hand, my fingers barely fit around him. I give his length a soft pump, and he snarls. The velvety heat of cock sears my palm. Bracing my free hand on his thighs, I look up at him. With our gazes locked, I slowly open my mouth and lick up his salty sweetness.

"Perfect," Ciaryn groans. "My perfect girl."

His praise washes over me. Liquid arousal pools between my legs and slides down my thighs. I give his head a soft kiss before tracing up the length of his shaft—Ciaryn's impressive muscles flex.

"I want you so bad," I moan. "For so long, I was afraid—of Timson, of my past—I didn't feel safe to be my true self. But you've freed me, and now I want to explore how deep this desire goes. This desire for you."

I trace my tongue along a pronounced vein. The taste of him makes my head spin.

"Whatever you want from me, you shall have, Stella." His eyes bore into mine. "You are a gift—my gift. And I'll never stop being grateful for you."

Warmth spreads throughout my body, and that's the last bit of encouragement I need. Opening wide, I take him fully into my mouth. Ciaryn's growl echoes through the forest around us. His claws spear through the grass and dirt at his sides.

My jaw stretches to accommodate his large size. Saliva pools in my mouth and dribbles down my chin as I suck him hard. Bracing my hands on his thighs, I bob my head along his hard cock. Taking him deeper each time, it's not long before I feel his length tickling the back of my throat. My eyes water, but I keep going, determined to watch Ciaryn fall apart in the same way he makes me.

"Good girl," Ciaryn growls. "Look at how well you take my cock into your little mouth. Even when it's too much, you keep going, don't you?"

"Yes." The word is garbled around his cock.

I gently skim my teeth along him, and he snarls. His hands fall to my head and tighten into my scalp. Gently he encourages me to suck him faster. Ciaryn's hips rise from the ground to meet my waiting mouth. I feel his claws pricking my scalp as he plunges further into me. I hold him in my mouth until I gag.

Pulling back, I watch a pool of saliva spill from my mouth and coat his hard cock.

Licking down his shaft, my tongue stops just before the large ridge at the base of his cock. It is more engorged than before.

"Stella," he snarls. "I'm close. Are you going to let me come in your mouth, mate?"

Mate. The word causes me to shiver.

I nod eagerly. I lick his slit before nipping and sucking back down his cock. When I reach the ridge again, taste it with a firm tongue. Ciaryn growls, his whole body going taut.

His reaction is all the encouragement I need to lick him there again. This part of him seems primal. An addition that is as foreign as it is arousing. Ciaryn snarls each time I do, his stomach muscles flexing under his dark fur.

"Naughty little thing you are," Ciaryn growls. "Tempting me to knot you when I haven't even told you what it means."

"Knot?" I ask as my lips skim along his ridge. "What's that?"

"It's something only alpha males get. That thing at the base of my cock is called a knot. Its purpose is to keep you locked to me when I fill you with my seed, heightening the chances of you becoming pregnant."

The image in my mind blazes brightly: my stomach round, Ciaryn by my side, holding me close, ready to protect me and our unborn child. Any apprehension I may have about the idea melts as the warmth of the image washes through me.

Without a moment of hesitation, I take him fully into my mouth again as my hand falls to his knot. I gently massage the hard mass while my mouth sucks him. Ciaryn snarls, his hands cupping my head as I work him deeper.

"Stella, fuck—I'm close."

"Come in my mouth," I say around his cock. "I want to taste you."

Ciaryn's eyes go wholly black, and every muscle in his body

tightens. I suck him once, twice, and on the third time, I take him deep as his hips lift to meet my mouth. Ciaryn roars as his seed floods my mouth. I swallow it down as quickly as I can. There is so much that it seeps between my lips and dribbles down my chin.

The salty taste of his come turns me obscenely slippery between my legs.

His cock jerks but spills nothing more, and that's when I gently release him from between my lips. A mixture of saliva and his spend spills from my mouth and slides down to my chest. Ciaryn raises into a sitting position. His massive chest moves rapidly up and down as he stares at me. One of his fingers curls into a lock of my hair.

"Stella, that was—I don't have the words. You're perfect," he says. "I made a mess of you. Let me bathe you."

His hands reach for me, but I shake my head. My hand is still around his cock, and I gently trace his knot. It hasn't gone down at all. Even his cock is hardening once more in my grip.

"I don't want a bath." My grip on him tightens. "I want you inside of me."

"Stella," he groans. "If I knot you—there is no undoing it. You're my mate forever. If the day came that you wanted to leave me, I couldn't let you go. We would be bonded forever. I refuse to keep you by force."

His eyes soften as he strokes my cheek.

"Are you sure you want my knot, knowing what it entails?"

Dropping his cock, I lean up and wrap my arms around his neck. With all the strength that I have, I roll us until I am flat on my back beneath him. The cool grass tickles my heated skin. The night sky looms above us, and the moon is impossibly full. Ciaryn's pine scent invades my lungs. Spreading my legs wider to accommodate him, I watch as his nostrils flare as he scents my arousal.

"I know what I want. I told you as much in the cottage." My

chest rises and falls with anticipation. "You are my heart—I cannot imagine my life without you. Bind me to you, mate."

With a growl, Ciaryn's mouth descends on mine. His lips are firm as they press against mine. His tongue licks against me, and I open my lips eagerly. In a moment, our tongues are tangling, fighting each other until I surrender to his dominance. I moan into his mouth, and my hands fall to his back.

The longer we kiss, the more incessant my need becomes. One of his hands falls to my chest, palming my breast gently. He worries the nipple until it's a stiff peak. His mouth leaves mine to taste my other breast. Ciaryn alternates his attention on each. My hips lift in invitation—seeking any friction I can find.

My wolfman releases my breast with a pop. He stares into my eyes as his hand trails lower. Parting me, he snarls at the wetness he finds there. His claw gently nudges my entrance, and I suck in a breath.

"Are you sure?" he asks again.

"Will it hurt?"

His nod is sharp.

"A bit at first—but not for long. Part of my knot's purpose is to provide you pleasure."

His claw tickles my clit, and I suck in a breath. Reaching between us, I wrap my hand around his cock and guide it towards my entrance. Lifting my hips, I capture his lips with mine.

"Then claim me, Ciaryn. Make it so we are never apart again."

With our lips still connected, Ciaryn knocks my hand away, and his head pushes into my entrance. The burn is already intense, and he's barely inside. I'm so wet I can tell he's fighting not to slide fully into me in one go. He continues his entrance on a slow thrust. Once he is fully inside me, I moan into his mouth. There is a pinch of pain, and I cry against him.

His lips leave mine to whisper encouragement and praise into my ears.

It feels like an eternity later when I feel his knot pressing into me. Taking a deep breath, I tighten my hold on his back as I feel the knot breach my entrance—stretching me wider than I thought possible. It steals my breath. Ciaryn's muscles are taut as he remains still inside me, allowing me to accommodate his size.

"Stella," he whispers. "Are you well?"

I nod, my eyes still closed tightly. Ciaryn begins to press soft kisses to my cheeks and forehead. His claw gently rubs my clit. After a few moments, the pain dissipates. Blinking my eyes open, I find Ciaryn's burning gaze staring down at me. Gently, he circles his hips. With his knot inside of me, he can't thrust fully but rather allow the fullness of his cock to heighten my pleasure.

"In time, I'll give you the fucking you deserve," he says as if reading my mind. "For your first time, I wanted to tie you to me."

"Ciaryn," I sigh. "This is—I—"

Words become lost as any lingering discomfort flees and pleasure consumes me. Despite the lack of movement, he still manages to fill me expertly. It's as if the size of him is enough to bring me to incomparable heights of pleasure. His hips flex, and it feels as if he is expanding inside of me. His claw continues to work my clit as my eyes threaten to roll back in my head.

"Your pussy is perfect, Stella. Just as you are. Look at how well you've taken all of me." His eyes begin to glow anew. "No one will ever have you like this. You are mine. *Forever*."

"Yes," I moan. "Forever."

Another tug on my clit causes my climax to barrel towards me. I clamp around his cock, straining with the onslaught of pleasure. Ciaryn grits his teeth as he absorbs my pleasure.

Instead of it beginning to subside, it feels like my body is racing towards another peak.

Wave after wave of pleasure crashes over me. Ciaryn licks down my neck and tastes each of my nipples. My fingernails shred his back as another climax bursts out of me. My wetness seeps from our joined bodies and soaks the grass below me. My mouth is open in a silent scream. Words are nothing more than a flurry of incoherent sounds.

Ciaryn rolls his hips one final time, and a torrent of his hot seed floods me. My body clamps around his jerking cock. This climax is more prolonged than the others. I feel him fill me to bursting with his come. His cock gives one final jerk, but he stays sealed to me. His knot hardens, keeping all of his spend locked within me.

Gently, my wolfman nuzzles my neck. My muscles feel weak. I never would have imagined this feeling. Total satisfied, my arms lazily wrap around his neck, bringing his body flush with mine. His fur tickles my hard nipples as we kiss gently.

My body trembles as he locks his arms around me.

"Stella, are you alright?"

Even with my blurry vision, I see the concern in his golden eyes.

"That was—I don't have the words for it."

Ciaryn trails kisses down my cheek and jaw.

"We'll be sealed like this for some time. Let me make you more comfortable."

My stomach growls, reminding me how little I've had to eat today. I'm hungrier now than I can ever remember being. Ciaryn locks his arms around me and drags me closer to the fire without separating us.

"I need to take better care of you. Let me feed you, mate. Then I'll give you another bath in the river."

"That sounds lovely."

Ciaryn removes the rabbits from the open flames. They're a

little burnt, but I can hardly blame him. I was a bit of a distraction. I take the cooked meat and eagerly devour it despite my usual aversion.

My wolfman watches me closely. With him still buried inside of me as I eat the food he's prepared, he doesn't have to tell me what he's thinking. I already know—I feel it, too. I'll tell him soon enough. For now, I tuck into Ciaryn's side and let him hold me, feeling happier than ever.

8

———

CIARYN

Is there anything more perfect than the feeling of Stella wrapped in my arms?

My cock is still buried deep inside of her. It will be a while before the knot releases. Claiming my mate for the first time had been beyond words. The feeling of her tight cunt urging me to spill inside of her caused my fangs to ache. Soon enough, I'll ask to mark her as mine—to leave a scar on her delicate shoulder to proclaim proudly that she belongs to me.

For now, I am content holding her supple body against my chest as she relaxes atop me. The glowing fire casts her in soft shadows while highlighting the golden strands of her hair.

Having ensured she was full from the rabbits I caught, we both enjoyed the comfortable silence, basking in our new bond. How is it that we have only known each other briefly, yet I feel her imprinted on my heart? She is embedded in the very fabric of my soul.

Stella is my mate.

I can hardly believe my good fortune that a male like me could be given such a precious gift. There is no denying our bond. My knot would not have formed for her, nor would her scent have drawn me close to her village those nights ago. I had been looking for her even if I hadn't known it then. Now that I have her, I'm eager to learn as much about my new mate as possible.

My claws skim down her smooth back as she snuggles in closer.

"Tell me more about you," I whisper.

Stella's blue eyes meet mine, a wicked gleam dancing in them.

"That sounds like something you should've said before coming inside me. We wasted no time, did we?"

I bark a laugh before kissing her pink cheek.

"I can think of no better time to learn more about my mate than when my cock is still deep within her perfect pussy."

Stella flushes bright red and buries her face in my neck.

"Don't get shy on me now," I murmur.

"What do you wish to know?" Her words are muffled against my fur.

"Anything," I say. "Everything."

Stella remains quiet for a moment. My hands drift down her back. Smoothing over her backside and traveling back up her spine. After a few more seconds trickle by, she raises her head from my shoulder. Unease dances in her eyes as she takes a deep breath.

"Would you believe me if I told you I was a princess?"

My ears flatten as I raise a brow. Her lips twist at the confession.

"Long ago, my name was Princess Caryssa of Enshire."

"Enshire?" I repeat, searching her lovely face. "Never heard of it."

"Good," she breathes. "It's far from here and a place I'd never wish for anyone to go."

I tuck a strand of dark golden hair behind her ear.

"Caryssa," I say. She wrinkles her delicate nose.

"I hated that name. My parents only chose it to compliment my brother, Carysen. A wicked man. I've heard whispers that he's dead, and I pray they are true."

I blink at her candor—at the harshness of her voice. Her brother must be cruel if someone as kind as her wishes for his death. I gently cup her cheek, skimming my thumb over her soft skin.

"To me, you'll always be Stella."

Her smile is brilliant. It chases away the darkness lingering in her gaze.

"That's all I've ever wanted. To be my own person. To belong somewhere—and to someone of my choosing." Her hand rests atop mine. "That's why I escaped."

"Escaped?"

Protectiveness crowds my chest at the thought of her being ill-treated. It makes sense. The situation must have been dire if she had to travel so far from her father's kingdom and change her name. Still, I can't help but hold her tighter, reminding her of my protection.

"My father—the King—wanted me married off. My mother only sought to serve him, so she was no advocate for me. That is why I was locked in my room until they could find an appropriate match for me. The day I left, my mother had come to inform me that my betrothal was imminent. If I did not comply, they would throw me into the dungeons. Before she left, my mother's parting words were that I'd be better off with the rodents."

A growl slips from between my clenched lips—red hazes over my vision. Every nerve in my body is on high alert. The story she has just recounted breaks my heart for her but also makes me all the more grateful to have found her. If she had not been brave enough to escape, our paths never would've crossed. The need to remind myself she is with me burns hot in my veins.

"You will be safe with me always. No one will harm you again. I'll kill anyone who comes for you," I vow.

Stella smiles as her hands tangle in the fur of my chest.

"I appreciate that, but I suspect no one is looking for me. It's been ten years, and I've heard barely a whisper of my father or his kingdom. Besides, you're taking me somewhere deep in *The Woods*. None of his guards would dare brave that for an inconsequential runaway princess."

"Nothing about you is inconsequential."

A fresh blush blooms on her cheeks. Her smile is soft and tender.

"Enough of this sad tale. I'd rather speak about our future. Tell me more about where you are taking me, mate."

Mate. The word kindles in my blood, and my soul reaches for hers. Even though we are tied together, a part of me still wants us to be closer.

"Like I said before, I don't know what kind of reception awaits us. My father passed away a short while ago, and I left immediately after. I'm sure they'll have questions for me—someone may even have taken my place in my absence. They could turn on me."

The thought is unpleasant but not out of the realm of possibility. A pack without an alpha cannot operate for long. One particular wolf has been eyeing my father's place for years, and I just gave him a perfect opportunity.

Stella inhales sharply.

"Don't worry, mate. Nothing will happen to you, I swear it. If they turn me away, I will find us a new home to call our own. I promise you."

"I don't want you getting hurt."

"I have to go back and face them. To honor my father at the very least." The fire burns low behind her. "You should rest. We'll reach the den by early afternoon."

Finally, the knot has gone down enough that I can withdraw from her. Stella inhales sharply at the loss of our connection. Our rush of mingling releases leaks from her and falls to the grass below. She shudders, and I roll her in my arms, fully cocooning her in my warmth.

Stella's spine molds to my front, and my head rests atop hers. A soft yawn slips from between her full lips.

"Goodnight, Ciaryn."

"Goodnight."

With a final deep breath, she fully relaxes. It is not long before I feel her breathing evenly in my arms. I can hear the steady pounding of her heart. I let it soothe me to sleep, all the while silently vowing to Stella that I'll always provide and protect her no matter what the future holds.

Forever.

9

———

STELLA

The den does not come into view until late the following evening.

Despite Ciaryn's assurances that we would reach it shortly after midday, an unexpected tryst this morning caused a considerable delay. Not that I'm complaining. Despite the stiffness of my muscles due to our traveling and the delicious soreness between my thighs, I can't help but feel blissfully content. A part of me had always felt adrift—an outsider even when I tried my best to settle. Now that the frayed parts of my soul are mended, I feel complete in a way I never had before.

However, I will admit that the closer we travel to the den, the more apprehension tickles the back of my neck. We are nestled deep within *The Woods*, a place I was taught to fear as a child—now it will become my new home.

The trees grow together densely, nearly blotting out the darkening sky above. The air is dank with the smell of grass and rotting foliage. Underneath the wet smell is Ciaryn's familiar scent.

I lay my cheek against his back, allowing the scent of pine

to wash over me. It is odd to think of my heart as no longer my own. Ciaryn has laid claim to every part of me. Our souls fused while he was tied to me last night. Baring the secrets of my past to him has lifted that phantom weight from my shoulders.

He met my confession with love and protection. Love is such a strong, fickle emotion. Many believe it takes time to form, but that is not the case. I do not need to spend weeks or months with Ciaryn to arrive at the conclusion I've already come to. I love him.

I will tell him soon enough—once this matter of his pack is settled.

The moon is in full bloom above us. Small animals scurry in the trees, and birds call overhead before perching on low-hanging branches.

A lone howl cuts through *The Woods*. Ciaryn's steps slow as we approach the mouth of a great cave. What lurks behind its rocky opening is entirely obscured by unending darkness. A shadow darts across my peripheral vision, and Ciaryn pauses a few feet from the entrance.

Another deep howl echoes from before us. My hands tangle into his fur as my heart pounds in my chest. There is a beat of silence before a striking pair of eyes beams from inside the opening. At first, there is only one, then after another moment, two, then three, appear. It is not long until the cavern is filled with countless pairs of glowing eyes.

Sleek, furry bodies hustle out in formation, encircling us.

Sharp, white teeth are bared from between ruby lips. Each one is heavily muscled. Their posture is tight, as if ready to pounce on us at any moment. None of them are as large as Ciaryn, but their sheer number makes sweat slide down my neck.

One of them growls at us, and Ciaryn answers in kind, his ears flattening. Despite my death grip on his fur, he gently slides me from his body and tucks me firmly against his side.

Dragging his gaze away from the wolfmen before us, he looks at me intently.

"Stay behind me. I'll keep you safe."

The words are low and end with a firm kiss to my brow. An uneasy whine echoes around us as Ciaryn turns to face the other wolfmen. It is clear that he rules over them. Even if they are displeased to see him, their bodies submit to the power he radiates. A few try to fight it, but the longer Ciaryn bares his fangs at them, the more they supplicate to his will.

One wolfman, however, shakes off Ciaryn's dominance. He strides forward, raising himself from all fours to his full height. His fur is a deep brown. One of his ears is bitten, missing a chunk as if lost in a fight. The scars smattering across his snout add to his intimidating appearance. I shuffle further behind Ciaryn when the other wolf's golden eyes land on me with a feral gleam. Ciaryn's warning growl vibrates throughout *The Woods*.

"You've returned," the other wolfman snarls.

"I have."

Despite Ciaryn's warning, his eyes dip to me again, and he licks over his sharp teeth.

"And with a human."

The muscles of Ciaryn's back tense.

"She is my mate." A few wolfmen look at each other before flattening their ears. "And as the alpha's mate, she will be permitted entrance into the den and live amongst us."

"She bears no claiming mark." Another wolfman with a white stripe down his back steps forward and nods toward me. "Will you dishonor us by not only abandoning your pack but now with lies?"

I look up at Ciaryn, waiting for him to explain, but he keeps his eyes locked on those circling us.

"My mate will bear my mark soon enough," Ciaryn spits.

"Why should we follow you?" The brown wolfman asks.

Ciaryn bares his fangs, lowering to his haunches.

"If you wish to challenge me for alpha, Lukar, I will oblige you. You've been dying to fight me since we were pups."

The brown wolfman—Lukar—bears his deadly fangs. Foamy saliva clings to the corners of his mouth and drops in frothy piles to the grass below.

My heart lurches in my chest. Ciaryn is strong—taller than the other male by a good foot—but he must be weary from our travels. Not to mention, he was injured by hunters only a few nights ago. I feel frozen to the spot, unable to make a sound. Whatever is passing between the two wolfmen must come to a head. The others in the pack seem to understand and take several steps back.

"If it is a challenge you want, it is a challenge you shall have." Lukar's lips pull into a sinister grin. "You are no alpha. You are weak, just as your father had been."

Without so much as a growl, Ciaryn launches himself into the air and lands atop the other wolfman. From there, a fight ensues unlike any I've ever seen before. I'd witnessed a few drunken brawls at the Wolf's Fang. Men come to blows over such small slights: a stolen sheep, spilling a cup of ale, or even perceived liberties they believe another has taken with their wife.

This clash is much different. The two males locked in a fury of shredding claws and snapping jaws are predators. Their moves are deadly—inflicting as much pain on the other as possible. Neither one shows any sign of yielding. This is a fight to the death.

Ciaryn's claws snag Lukar in the side, drawing blood. The metallic scent coats the air. It wakes me from my daze and urges me to move. The other pack members venture closer to the action, taking in the grisly scene, but I want to be as far away as possible. It only now strikes me that Ciaryn could be killed. Coldness settles over my skin.

No, he will not perish here—he can't. I only just found him, and now he is facing another brush with death. I want to rush into the carnage and urge Ciaryn to stop. We don't need a pack—we would be happy, just the two of us.

My heart nearly stops as Lukar's jaws lock around Ciaryn's forearm. The pained howl of my mate causes my knees to buckle. Quickly, he manages to shake off his opponent, but blood flows down his arm. The other wolfman knocks him off his feet, and they grapple with each other. Dirt and grass fly around them in a frenzy.

I take a small step forward, arm extended. Before I can take another, I sense a presence at my side.

"They must do this," a soft voice says.

Glancing beside me, I take in the large gray wolf with sparkling blue eyes a few feet away. The ends of his fur are nearly white, giving me the impression that he is much older than the other wolfman in the pack. He nods towards the two clashing wolves who are once more on their feet. Blood streams out of Lukar's mouth, and Ciaryn limps as they circle each other.

"Lukar will never accept Ciaryn as his alpha without this duel. If he still refuses to submit to his authority, Ciaryn must kill him." At my sharp inhale the older wolf's eyes soften. "It is our way."

"It seems so brutal," I say.

The older wolfman nods.

"In time, you will understand how we live."

A sharp whine causes me to whip my head back towards the fighting. Despite them both being covered in blood, Ciaryn has managed to pin Lukar beneath him. The brown wolfman's arm is bent at a grotesque angle. Ciaryn snaps his jaws at the other wolfman, his black fur shining in the moonlight.

"Do you yield?" my mate snarls.

Lukar thrashes in his grip, but it is to no avail. Ciaryn has him beaten. They both know it. With a resounding growl, Ciaryn tightens his grip on his shattered arm.

"Do you yield?" he repeats.

With a broken yelp, Lukar ceases his movements.

"Yes," he spits, blood trailing from his mouth.

Ciaryn snarls again.

"Alpha," Lukar adds, infusing as much hate into the title as he can muster.

With one final snarl, Ciaryn releases the other wolfman man and rises to his feet. There is a soft murmuring amongst the crowd. His golden eyes scan his pack as if daring another to issue a challenge. When none do, he nods.

"Let Lukar lick his wounds." The wolves around him bow their heads in supplication. "And let us have no further discussion on the matter. I am your alpha—now until I take my last breath. Those who wish to challenge that fact can look to Lukar as an example of what will happen if you do. Next time, I will not be so generous as to let you live."

"Yes, alpha," rings out from the gathered crowd.

They part for him as he turns, nodding in reverence in his presence. His eyes find mine, and his whole body loses its rigidity. Clearly relieved that I am unharmed, even though I was not the one locked in battle. Limping over to me, the gore coating his body makes my heart ache. I understand why he had to do this, but I still don't like it.

He runs a hand over my cheek, and I melt at his touch.

"Are you alright?" he asks.

"I should be asking you that." I look pointedly at his blood-soaked fur. "But I already know the answer."

"Nothing time won't heal." He draws me towards him, and I go willingly. "But I would prefer my healing done by your masterful hand."

"I'm sure you would." I smile before leveling a stern look at him. "I understand why you had to do this, but I don't want to see you hurt like this again. Understand?"

"Demanding little thing you are," Ciaryn chuckles.

"You should know that well by now, mate."

The glow in Ciaryn's eyes says he knows precisely how needy I can be. His mouth descends on mine in a brush of lips. It is far too chaste, and I'm eagerly parting my lips for his tongue to sweep inside. I hold tightly to his chest, my hands turning sticky with his blood. We'll both need to bathe tonight, but I need his taste above all else. It is a reminder that he is alive and we've overcome this first challenge against our future.

A soft throat clearing causes my cheeks to go up in flames. I had completely forgotten that we weren't alone. Breaking off the kiss, I turn towards the other wolfman. His blue eyes dance with amusement.

"Brydon," Ciaryn says roughly.

"Happy to see you, Ciaryn. I'm too old to be playing alpha. I hope that your arrival here is a permanent one."

"It is," Ciaryn says, tucking me into his side.

"Good." He nods towards me. "Take care of her."

"Always," Ciaryn vows.

Without another word, the older wolf saunters towards the den's opening and disappears into the darkness. Ciaryn's hand snags mine. Pressing a kiss to the back of my palm, his golden eyes burn me alive.

"Let me take you home, Stella."

Without warning, he lifts me into his arms. I squeal as I cling to him. The small satchel containing my belongings hangs limply at my side. I'll have to learn where the nearest town is to find more healing supplies. As well as the contraceptive herbs—at least for a time. I wouldn't mind a family, but I'd like it to be Ciaryn and me for a bit.

Darkness surrounds us as we pass through the cave's opening. Wolfmen can see better in the dark than humans because

Ciaryn navigates us expertly through the den. After a bit, a faint glow greets us. It illuminates the smooth stone walls and steps carved into the cavern. All is quiet the deeper we go; most of the pack must be exhausted from the return of their alpha.

Inside the caves are different alcoves, each belonging to a different pack member, Ciaryn explains. Once a wolfman finds his mate, that is where he and his family will live until the child is old enough for a dwelling of his own. Torches are placed outside each opening, casting them in golden light. We travel further into the waiting depths until we reach another alcove.

Ciaryn ducks inside the darkness. Settling me on my feet, I hear him shuffle around until one of the torches inside blazes to life. Despite his limp, he quickly lights the sconces and candles, and our room is awash in glowing light.

It is a modest room in a much more secluded area of the den. Inside is a small table with a few wooden bowls, a cupboard filled with jars and a few leather-bound books, and a smattering of metal utensils on the table. This room was set up for a human to reside in, for Ciaryn has no use for a spoon.

A large pallet rests in the center of the room, with silk sheets and pillows decorating its top. My weary muscles ache to lie on it after our travels.

"I'm sorry it is so bare," Ciaryn says beside me. "You, of course, can make any changes you'd like to. This is our home."

I smile at him, setting my satchel on the table with a thud.

"It's wonderful." I nod towards one of the empty chairs. "Now, let me take a look at your wounds."

Unwrapping some of my herbs, Ciaryn directs me to where to find fresh water. There is a soft trickling sound near the back of the alcove, and I'm delighted to see clear, flowing water. It is warm enough to bathe in. Quickly, I wash the blood from my hands and face before stripping out of my soiled gown. Scrubbing at the crimson stains, I leave them to dry along the edge of the small pool. Collecting a bowl of water, I return to Ciaryn.

His eyes dance as he takes in the bare skin of my arms. My shift is thin, and the air inside the dwelling is cool enough to have my nipples pebbling against the front. Kneeling before him, I wet a few clean cloths with water and cleaned the blood from his fur. Luckily, he has already begun healing. Most of the wounds have sealed closed and scabbed over. Still, I make him a quick concoction to ensure none of them fester.

Once satisfied, I allow Ciaryn to set about preparing our dinner. He apologizes that it's so meager—a few bits of dried meat and berries. He informs me that there is a small trading town a half day's journey from here. Tomorrow, he'll set out and gather everything we need. He leaves me briefly to bathe himself in the small stream at the back.

Ciaryn returns gloriously naked and dripping wet all over the stone floor. His scent deepens, causing me to turn slippery between my thighs. As well as the sight of his impressive cock stiffening between his legs. I shift in my seat at the table, desperate for relief. My mate's eyes glow, and I know he can sense my desperate state.

Quickly, he makes a fire in the small, carved hearth along the nearest wall. Once it is blazing, the room turns deliciously warm. Ciaryn shakes himself dry before holding out a hand to me. I take it, allowing him to lay me down in the pile of silk and feathers. The fire licks over my skin.

Resting on his side, Ciaryn's hand glides over my face, watching me intently. The silence stretches between us. Not uncomfortable, but heavy with unspoken admissions. Cupping my cheek, he turns my face towards him. His golden eyes are unreadable.

"Do you fear me now, Stella?"

The question is asked so softly I nearly miss it.

"What?" Startled, I grip his hand in mine. "No. *No*, of course not."

"I couldn't stand it if you looked at me differently after what transpired between me and Lukar."

I nod.

"Truthfully, I detest the violence, but as I said before, I understand why you had to do it." I slide closer toward him on the pallet, our chest nearly brushing. "Just like with Timson, sometimes violence is the only answer."

"But that violence will never be directed at you," he states. "Never, Stella. I can't even imagine raising my voice at you."

I giggle at his serious face.

"Because I am perfect?"

"In every way," he agrees. "And you are mine."

Quirking an eyebrow, I purse my lips.

"Are you unsure of my devotion?" he asks.

He rolls me on top of him. Ciaryn's large hands find the backs of my leg and the hem of my shift. Slowly, he lifts it from my body, baring me completely to his hungry gaze. Tossing it aside, his tongue licks over my pert nipple, and I moan.

"If I have left you questioning the depth of my desire, let me rectify that now."

Alternating between both of my nipples, his large cock rises to attention and presses against my backside. My arousal seeps from me as I grind against his front. Claws sink into the fleshy swell of my ass, encouraging my hips to work faster. My breaths come out in little pants, desperate for release at my mate's hand.

"I don't doubt your devotion." I open my heavy-lidded eyes. "But I wonder why I don't bear this claiming mark the other wolves mentioned?"

Ciaryn releases my breast with a pop. His eyes are liquid fire as he stares at me. Gently, he rolls me onto my back. The soft silk is cool against my hot skin. Ciaryn looms above me. My thighs widen to accommodate his size, burning slightly from the stretch. His mouth descends on mine.

The kiss is claiming—a mixture of tongues and teeth locked in battle. Once he is satisfied in his plundering of my mouth, his lips leave mine to taste the skin of my neck. I suck down air, and my hands fall to his strong back. My fingers thread between his soft fur, locking him to me.

"The claiming mark," he purrs against me. "It is the final thing I have yet to bestow on you. It is a warning to all who see you that you are spoken for. That your mate shares your bed and safeguards your heart."

"Ciaryn," I sigh as his tongue licks the hollow of my throat.

"I'll bite you here, Stella." His teeth prick into my shoulder, not hard enough to break the skin. "And you'll beg me to do it."

"Yes," I say. "Bite me, my mate. My alpha."

Worry clouds his eyes.

"I still do not feel worthy of that title. I feel even less worthy of you, Stella. How could I be given someone so wonderful?"

"Because you are a good male, Ciaryn. The only male I've ever needed—or wanted."

I stare into his eyes and let him see all my love for him in my gaze.

"It won't be easy—the others are still wary of me, but I'll step up. I'll keep us safe. I promise you, mate."

"Of course you will," I agree. "Now, my great alpha, I have an ache that needs your attention."

Surprised by my boldness, I feel a blush dance on my cheeks. Ciaryn gives me a wicked grin, kissing me soundly. His mouth leaves mine in a slow descent down my body. He stops at my breasts, licking over each pink nipple in turn before traveling lower. His tongue dips into my navel before hefting my legs over his shoulders.

"It's been my greatest dream to have my mate share this room. I want your scent to cover everything." He inhales deeply, his ears flattening to his head. "As for your ache, let me attend to that first."

His mouth descends on my most intimate flesh. The fur of his cheeks tickles the inside of my thighs. His claws fall to my hips and keep me steady as his tongue licks up my slit. The lick is soft at first, and he moans at my taste. My hands fist the silk sheets as his tongue travels up me from top to bottom once more.

"Such a sweet little pussy," Ciaryn praises.

My mate's tongue spears into my entrance, and my back comes off the pallet. He thrusts that slick muscle in and out of me as his snout nuzzles my clit. Curling it expertly inside me, my breathing becomes ragged as my peak looms close.

The soreness of my muscles loosens the longer his mouth is on me. My hips move of their own accord, grinding against his face. Ciaryn chuckles, the vibration making my teeth clench. Wetness seeps from me and soaks the fur on his face. He alternates between nuzzling me and long licks of my wet flesh.

"Ciaryn," I sigh. "I'm close—"

My words end in a squeak as I feel his claw prod my back entrance. Gently dipping a finger into the tight ring of muscle, my breaths become ragged.

"Tight here too, mate. Will you let me lay claim to this hole as well?"

Words escape me, and all I can do is nod. Ciaryn chuckles.

"Let me make you come first before I get too greedy."

Wrapping his arms across my hips, he lifts my lower body off the sheets and holds me tight to his mouth. His tongue dives into me before he sucks my clit into his mouth. My muscles tense, and warmth spreads throughout my stomach. The ends of my vision begin to blur. The way he holds me gives me no reprieve; all I am left to do is weather the impending storm.

Ciaryn's teeth graze my clit, and my whole body erupts. I scream his name as he holds me through my climax. He licks me through it all, claiming every drop of my pleasure. When I am nothing more than a quivering mess, he lowers me back to the sheets. His mouth meets mine, sharing my musky flavor.

His hard cock pokes between my thighs as if seeking entrance into its newfound home. I wrap my hand around his length, pumping him a few times in my tight grip. I notice his knot is not as rigid as before. Looking up at him, I raise a brow. Ciaryn smirks before leaning down and resting his lips on my ear.

"Trust, mate, I will knot you again tonight. But first, I must make good on my previous promise and fuck you." His teeth skim over my throat. "Isn't that what you want, Stella? To be pounded by my cock?"

"Yes," I whimper. His wanton words cause more arousal to leak out of me. "Please, Ciaryn—mate—fuck me."

He chuckles, taking his cock from my hand and lining it up with my entrance.

"Be careful what you wish for, Stella. I fear it will be a rare occurrence when my cock is not deep inside your pretty cunt. It's already been too long since last I was inside you, wouldn't you agree?"

"Yes, yes!"

The head of his cock presses into my opening. Slowly, he slides in, meeting no resistance. The familiar stretch burns, but there is no pain. There is only the obscene decadence of his massive cock skimming along my inner walls. Already my climax looms as his cock butts up against my womb. His dark, velvety flesh disappears completely inside me. His knot remains just outside, still not fully engorged.

Ciaryn retreats his hips before thrusting into my waiting depths. I cry out at the intensity, my nails raking down his back. Ciaryn growls and thrusts again. His pace is slow, but each pounding of his cock steals my breath. His pine scent wraps around me, as does the unmistakable smell of our coupling. It is heady and spurs me to lower my hands to his ass and encourage him to take me faster.

Understanding what I want without speaking, Ciaryn's hands fall to the sides of my head as he powers into me. His thrusts speed up, turning sloppy but still reaching deep. The head of his cock brushes a spot deep inside of me that causes my hips to raise and meet his thrusts full-on.

"Look at how well you take me, Stella. Your body was made for me."

"It's yours," I pant. "Always."

"I'll be the envy of every male, for they will never know such pleasure."

He continues to fuck me without reprieve. My walls begin to tighten around him as warmth trickles through my veins. His knot has hardened with each thrust, becoming hard to ignore. Lifting my head, I capture his mouth, threading my fingers around his skull. His pace never falters. His tongue thrusts into my mouth in time with his hips.

"Ciaryn," I whisper. "Bite me."

His eyes flash as I lower his head to my shoulder.

"Stella—"

"Bite me!" I scream.

Without another word, he pounds me ruthlessly. My ass smacks off the cradle of his hips. The sound of our bodies slapping together echoes around the room. His finger finds my clit and gently massages it. That's the last bit of encouragement my body needs as it erupts. The pleasure of my cascading orgasm lessens as his teeth sink into my shoulder.

His sharp fangs pierce my skin just as his hard knot pushes inside me. My scream of pleasure turns into a yelp of pain. Ciaryn's teeth hold firm, and so does his knot. He rotates his hips, and a fresh wave of pleasure washes over me and eradicates any discomfort. Rocking inside of me, another climax is set off almost immediately.

As if satisfied his mark will hold, he releases my shoulder. Licking at the wound, I watch my blood decorate his tongue. I moan at the sight and open my mouth for his kiss. The metallic taste causes another orgasm to roll through me.

Can a woman die from too much pleasure? If anyone were to know, it would be me.

"Stella, Stella, *Stella*." Ciaryn whispers my name like a prayer.

"Ciaryn," I respond, my muscles loose. I feel like I'm floating on a cloud. "Come inside me, my mate. Seal me to you."

With a mighty roar, Ciaryn does just that. His warm seed floods me, filling me while his knot holds it deep inside of me. Once he is spent, his head falls to my shoulder. Gently, he kisses his claiming bite before looking at me.

"I am well," I say before he can ask me.

Ciaryn smiles and holds me tight as he rolls us onto his back. Tucking me under his chin, our rapid breathing is the only sound in the small room. He drags a sheet over our quivering bodies as I rest my head on his chest. I feel our hearts beating in time, solidifying our bond even further.

10

CIARYN

Stella is sleeping soundly when I wake the next morning. I take in her slumbering form and again marvel at my good fortune. She is lovely. The dark golden strands of her hair are fanned out behind her. The freckles on her cheeks look like stars. Her pale skin is smooth and flushed. Only a hint of her breasts are bared by the silk sheet still wrapped around her.

My savage bite mars her delicate shoulder. The scar will be prominent. Self-satisfaction ripples through me at the physical proof of my claim. With my come still in her pussy and my bite on her shoulder, there is no question she has been thoroughly and completely mated.

Memories of last night come rushing back. She is such a responsive mate. Coaxing her to climax does not take long, and that pleases me greatly. My knot had released a few hours ago and allowed me to slip from her body. She had awoken briefly, but I mollified her with a kiss, and she was sleeping soundly once more.

Despite having spent much of the night inside her, my cock and knot are coming alive to claim her again. Now that she is my mate and has been welcomed into the den, everything is different. To keep Stella safe, I must step up and lead the pack. I have their submission as their alpha, but I long for their respect. Once I secure it, they will be loyal not only to me but to Stella as well.

I will be a worthy alpha to my pack just as I will be a worthy male to my mate. Stella is worth the effort. I will strive to make it so she never regrets choosing me and forsaking her human life. She will want for nothing, and I will see to all her needs.

Possessiveness floods my chest, and I wrap her tightly in my arms. Her backside brushes my hard cock, and she shifts against me with a sleepy moan. Slowly, her blue eyes blink open and find mine. She smiles lazily, turning towards me in the cradle of my arms.

"Morning," she sighs.

I kiss her softly before pulling back.

"How are you feeling?" I ask, skimming my claws down her spine.

"Sore," she admits with a wrinkle of her nose. "You are quite the vigorous and demanding lovemaker."

I chuckle softly, pressing my forehead against hers.

"How can I not be with a mate as perfect as you? I'm only loving you as thoroughly as you deserve."

Stella inhales softly, her eyes going wide.

"You—you love me?"

My eyes bore into hers, letting her glimpse the depths of my soul.

"From the moment you saved me from those hunters, you have owned my heart. Honestly, maybe even before when I caught your scent on the wind and ventured too close to your village." I kiss her soft brow. "I love you more than anything in this world."

Salt perfumes the air, and I glance down to see Stella's eyes rimmed with red.

"Ciaryn, I—"

A sharp howl echoes through the den. The sound of unease causes my ears to perk up and my lips to curl into a snarl. My head whips towards the opening of our dwelling. With my heightened hearing, I can make out the sounds of claws clicking along the stone floor and heading toward the den's entrance.

"What's going on?" Stella asks

"I don't know, but it doesn't sound good," I say, kissing her lips. "Stay here."

Sliding on an old pair of shorts, I prowl down the corridor and charge towards the front of the den. A few members of the pack fall into step beside me, nodding in respect as we hustle towards the front of the cavern.

"Who raised the alarm?" A young wolfman named Puk asks me.

"I have no idea."

We hustle as a unit until we meet up with the other pack members. I nod to the others gathered around me. Brydon meets my eye with concern, lifting his snout towards the clearing awash in the morning sun. A quick head count tells me the whole pack is present except for one: Lukar.

Remaining in darkness, I peer into the clearing. The brown wolfman is easy enough to locate. A brigade of twelve heavily armed human hunters stand in a line a few feet from our den. A bruised and battered Lukar lays bound at their feet. After a few moments, the lead hunter steps forward and unholsters his gun.

He isn't a particularly tall man, but the arsenal of his weaponry makes him a threat. Silver bullets drape along his chest, as well as a smattering of silver knives glinting at his hips. The others of his hunting party are dressed similarly. His dark hair is greased back from his face, exposing beady eyes and pockmarked cheeks. Thin lips peel back to reveal chipped yellow teeth.

"We know you're in there!" he calls. "Hand over the girl, and we'll let him go."

His worn boot connects soundly with Lukar's ribs—the wolf grunts and curls in on himself.

"Found your friend here all alone in *The Woods*. Had to use a little force, but he told us where you were in time." The hunter chuckles. "Also told us of the girl you've taken. She matches the description of the one we've been hired to bring back. Her boss told us she'd never willingly go with you lot, and after we found those bodies at her place, well..."

He trails off. None of my pack makes a move. From the steam coming from Lukar's wounds, I can tell they used silver on him. Under that type of pain, I can't fault him for confessing even as red settles over my vision. If these hunters want Stella, they'll have to get through me. I will never hand her over—I'd rather die.

"Just give her to us, and we'll go." The man kicks Lukar again, and my teeth grind together. "Or we'll kill him and put a bullet in each one of you."

The others bear their teeth at the threat, and I follow them. Inhaling deeply, I let Stella's sweet scent calm me. Lowering onto my haunches, I'm ready to strike. The others follow my lead, ready to pounce once I give the command. Stella is pack, and no one will take her from us.

"Alright, have it your way," the hunter sighs. "I'll count to ten. Produce the girl, or I'll shoot him."

He trains his long gun on Lukar's head. The male gives a whine, pulling at the silver-laced ropes tethering him. These are experienced hunters who won't go down without a fight.

"One," the hunter calls. "Two. Three. F—"

"Wait!" A familiar voice echoes in the cavern behind us.

There is a flash of gold before I register Stella's petite frame running headlong through the den's opening. She breaks through our lines before anyone can grab her and stands exposed in the clearing. I don't think about my safety and rush towards her side. She whirls towards me, shaking her head and urging me to stay back.

I do as she says, even if I am in agony. Every protective instinct I have is screaming at me to grab her and haul her back into the safety of the den. Brave and beautiful, Stella shows no fear as she turns towards the under. Her gown is unlaced as if she merely threw it on and left. It hangs from her shoulders and drags on the ground.

My mark is on full display in the morning sun. It doesn't escape the hunter's notice. Their lustful gazes on her soon give way to disgust. The lead hunter points his gun at her, and she holds up her delicate hands.

"You need to leave this place. Tell Old Bill I was not kidnapped but came here of my own volition."

The leader sketches a brow before laughing in disgust.

"You can't expect us to believe that girl. Look at that mark—surely you didn't ask for that. Bad enough, one of these beasts has already rutted upon you." He spits on the ground. "You wish to remain with these animals?"

"Yes," she says clearly. "I love their alpha, and he loves me. This is where I'm meant to be."

My heart expands in my chest. To hear my mate claim me openly and boldly sets my blood on fire. If not for the present danger, I'd already be between her thighs, giving us both pleasure.

Her confession is met with a disgusted snarl by the lead hunter.

"Stupid girl. It is a pity that a pretty thing like you has been tainted." His finger tightens on the trigger. "And we don't need your belly growing with one of their pups and further polluting our land with their kind."

Stella inhales sharply, and I react in time, launching myself at the hunter. The sound of the gun firing barely registers as my jaw locks around his neck. Metallic blood coats my tongue as my fangs tear through flesh and muscles. With a mighty tug, I hear the cracking of bones and wrench the hunter's hand from his shoulders.

There is a fury of activity. Bullets fly as guns fire over and over before a member of my pack snuffs out each hunter. Screams echo around the clearing, and crimson blood soaks the grass and beds of fallen leaves. Limbs litter the clearing, and I spat the hunter's head onto the ground. Once the final hunter falls and Lukar is freed, I turn towards Stella, needing to feel her in my arms and assure myself she is safe.

At first all I can see is Stella's smile. How brittle it is causes my hackles to rise. Then I glance down and notice the blood blooming across her abdomen.

11

———

CIARYN

Stella sways on her feet, and I catch her before she can hit the ground.

I was unaware I had even moved until I'm cradling her small body in my arms. Her skin is sickly pale. She feels cold and clammy to the touch. I press my hand to her wound, and it is instantly wet with her blood. Her eyelids are heavy—her blinks are too long.

"Stella," I whisper hoarsely. "Stay awake. Keep your eyes open, please. Stella."

Her hand limply raises to my cheek, caressing it softly. The look of adoration in her eyes causes my heart to crack. Each breath is painfully shallow. I curl myself around her. Members of my pack have gathered close, each one whining and lowering on all fours.

"I love you, Ciaryn," she says softly. Tears fall down her round cheeks. "I always will."

I hold her close and howl up towards the sky. This cannot be happening. I just found her, and I've already lost her. She can't die. There has to be something I can do. Someone as wonderful as Stella should be saved. If there is any force out there, I silently beg for it to come and help her. I'll give anything for this not to be the end of us.

My heart shatters with each of her ragged breaths. I clutch her close, vowing that if she doesn't make it, neither shall I. I understand my father more now than I ever have. How had he lived thirty years without his mate? I don't know if I can bear even thirty seconds without her. My agony yawns open and threatens to swallow me whole.

Her body is cold as I howl once again. The sound shakes the trees above. My cries echo around me until I feel the ground beneath me rattling with despair. My body shakes with the force of my trembling. I can hardly stand it. I kiss her face, whispering words of love and devotion in her ears as the world around us ripples. I will my broken heart to kill me so that we can be reunited in whatever comes after this life.

Perhaps the ground will open and swallow us both.

A startled yelp goes up amongst our pack, and the wolves around me dig their claws into the grass. Only once their unease tickles my neck do I finally realize the ground is actually shaking. The trees around us wobble and pull back as the ground below us opens. Bright light spills up from beneath the crack in the soil—the pungent scent of fresh flowers and dank earth soaks the air.

From the crumbly ground, a lone figure appears.

Its skin is milky green, and its eyes are wholly black. A crown of gnarled branches rests over its brow. It's dressed in a silk skirt and matching pants. Its bare hands are black and tipped with deadly claws. I snarl at the intruder and haul Stella harder against me.

"What are you?" I demand. "Why are you here?"

If this is some demon that has come to spirit her soul away, I will slay him where he stands. No one is touching my mate—I refuse to let even death separate us.

The creature arches a delicate white brow.

"A friend," it replies simply.

In a flash of white light, he appears beside me. His long fingers glide over Stella's brow, and I snap my teeth at him and pull her away. The creature merely waves a hand, unperturbed by my threat.

"She's dying."

The blunt statement feels like being gutted by a silver knife. I look away, pressing another kiss to her cold brow. Her breaths are even fainter than before. The creature huffs beside me before rising to his full height and brushing invisible dirt from his pants.

"You wolves are such obstinate creatures. It's been ages since I dealt with one. Only for my blossom would I do something like this."

I narrow my eyes at him.

"Speak plainly," I spit.

Rolling his eyes, the creature extends a hand towards Stella.

"I will save your little mate."

Apprehension tickles the back of my neck. I've heard of creatures like this who live in *The Woods*. One's who bargain and make deals. One's who have power over life and death. My father warned me of such beings and to take care when dealing with them.

An offer like this is not given without repayment.

"Tick-tock, wolf. Her final breath draws nearer every moment." His dark eyes glow. "Saving her then won't be as simple."

"You can restore her to what she was before?"

The creature nods.

With a deep breath, I look down at Stella's face. I vowed to always protect her, and I meant it. Whatever this creature wants for his help I shall be the one to give it.

"I will take on the debt of this bargain." My voice is firm.

"That is not for you to decide." Before I can protest, he

waves another dismissive hand. "But lucky for you, this is repayment for the debt I owe your mate. She saved mine from a most unfortunate fate, and now I am here to do the same."

Shock renders me speechless. However, if a creature like this owes anyone a favor, it would be Stella. Her kindness knows no bounds. I would know, after all.

With a wave of the creature's hand, warm light envelopes Stella. The scent of flowers nearly blankets her honey scent. I watch in awe as color returns to her sallow cheeks. There is a soft clink as the bullet from her wound slips from her body, and the hole closes up. Her full lips part on a gasp, and she blinks wild blue eyes open at me.

"Ciaryn," she murmurs.

I say nothing but rain kisses all over her beautiful face. My lips touch every part of her, and I hold her close. Her warmth soaks into me as she clutches at my arms.

"Stella, Stella." I repeat her name as a reminder that she is here with me.

Turning towards the stranger still lingering beside us, I give him a nod.

"Thank you for saving her."

Stella's eyes widen as she takes in the figure. A small gasp leaves her when it smiles, exposing two sets of pointed teeth.

"Wolves live much longer than humans do. I fixed that little obstacle for you two as well."

It is my turn to gasp. Both of us share a look of bewilderment. That had been another point I meant to explain to her. Wolves can live hundreds of years, but most will bind their lives to their mates and grow old with them. My father had not been mated to my mother long enough to see it as a necessity yet, so he lingered without her.

Now, Stella and I no longer have to worry about that.

"And my thanks to you, Stella, for helping my Laurelle flee your brother all those years ago," the creature says with a smile.

"Helping you escape the castle and saving you tonight was the least I could do."

Stella's eyes widened. "That was y—"

Before she can finish, the creature is gone. The ground groans as it shuffles back into place and neatly knits over as if it had never opened in the first place. A calmness settles over the clearing.

I feel off-kilter as I hold Stella in my arms. In one moment, I was ready to will myself to die to be with her, and now the two of us have centuries to enjoy each other. We stare at each other, lost in the overwhelming sensation of our love. She turns in my lap, wrapping her arms around my neck.

My pack gathers around us, each member bloody from the fight. Our quarrel with the hunters seems so long ago. Stella frowns before looking over each of the wolfmen gathered there.

"I'm sorry to all of you for exposing myself like that. I just thought I had to try at least if there was a way to end this without bloodshed." She shakes her head. "Now I see that a show of force is necessary to keep our home and each other safe."

A great howl goes up, and they all bow their heads to my mate. I hold her close, rising with her in my arms, and nod to those around us.

"We will work on fortifying the den so that if any more hunters come looking for her—or any of us—they will be snuffed out swiftly."

"In the meantime," Stella says, grinning at me before approaching our pack. "I will tend to your wounds."

I want to argue and demand she go back to our room where I can keep a close eye on her and remind myself that she is very much alive. However, her look tells me she needs to do this. As mistress of the pack, these are her people, too, and tending to them will solidify her role here.

"Those less injured, stay with me to help strengthen our defenses."

I press a kiss to Stella's mouth and allow her to disappear into the den with a few of our most heavily wounded. The clearing empties quickly, with only Brydon and a few other wolves remaining to help set up traps.

A limping Lukar stumbles over to me. Blood still oozes from many of his wounds, and one of his eyes is swelling shut.

"Alpha," he says, spitting blood from his mouth. "I didn't mean to bring them here. It was foolish to go off alone, but I needed space to think. They tortured me. I—"

"All is well, Lukar," I say, touching his shoulder. "You need Stella's healing. As an important member of this pack, I want to see you well taken care of."

Lukar bows his head.

"Your mate is very brave, alpha." Longing dances in his eyes. "I hope to find my own one day."

"You will," I reassure him.

I look at the faces of the other wolves gathered. Even Brydon, who was a century older than my father, still has that same look of longing. I never understood why only my father had found his mate. It is a mystery that has plagued our pack for centuries.

Don't worry—I took care of that, too, says a voice on the wind. I shudder at the sound, but I feel comforted by it. For the first time in my life, there is true hope for the future—not just for Stella and me but for the pack as well.

"Trust me, I have a feeling you'll all find your mates very soon."

12

STELLA

The daylight had almost completely faded when I returned to our room.

Healing nearly twenty wolfmen was no easy task. While the attack by the hunters had been brief, the consequences were substantial. Injuries ranged from scrapes and bruises to large gashes and bones needing to be reset. My skills as a healer were tested, and I wouldn't be surprised if they vastly improved during my time here.

After all, I have centuries to practice them.

I shiver at the memory—at the creature who saved me, bound my life to Ciaryn's, and brought news that Laurelle made it to safety. It seems she and I have found happy endings with our monsters.

Speaking of my monster, even though I feel bone tired, my heart races the closer I get to our dwelling. Ciaryn checked in with me throughout the day to ensure I had eaten and drank enough water. He and those less injured spent the better part of the day setting traps outside the den and scouting to ensure no other hunting parties found their way here.

Despite the dire consequences that could've come from his

decision, my heart does ache for Old Bill. I should've sent word to him and not allowed him to believe I had gone missing. Once things have settled down and no more hunters come to our door, I'll find a way to get a letter to him.

However, the only thing I want now is to be back in my mate's arms.

My back and shoulders ache. Pain pounds through my head in a breathtaking rhythm. I want a bath, bed, and Ciaryn—not necessarily in that order.

The torches along the walls have been lit, guiding me towards our dwelling. After being put in one of the unoccupied alcoves to heal the others, I realize just how much larger our home is, fitting for the alpha and his mate. I wouldn't care if we shared a broom closet as long as I had him.

Though that decadent silk and pillow pile sounds ridiculously tempting at the moment.

I sag with relief as I finally make it to our room. The pallet has been turned down, and it looks inviting. A fire roars off to the side, keeping the room warm. My eyes take in the bare walls before landing on Ciaryn's handsome face. He looks just as weary as I do. Nevertheless, he jolts to life when he spies me and rises from his seat at the wooden table. Extending his hand towards me, I ran into his arms, allowing him to envelop me.

His nose dives into my hair, inhaling deeply. I fall against him, the last of my strength fading as the weight of today finally hits me. The silence in the room makes me realize we almost lost each other today. His hold on me tells me he's thinking the same thing—now that we are alone, it is easy to remember how bad today could've been.

Ciaryn purrs softly, and the vibrations tickle my cheek. I press my nose into his soft fur and inhale his comforting pine scent. We are alive—we have each other, and that is all that matters. I love him, and he loves me. My mortality has no bearing on our time together now, and our beautiful future unfurls before me, urging me to claim it with both hands.

My mate runs his large hands over my sore back and shoulders—his touch is firm. I have no doubt he too is reassuring himself that I am here. I look up at him and see the love kindling in his gaze.

"I'm fine, Ciaryn," I say, reaching up to cup his cheek.

His large body shudders at the slight touch.

"I've never felt fear like that before, Stella. It was the first time I truly understood the depth of my father's pain. If you are not in this world, then I have no place in it either."

Pressing up onto my toes, I place a soft kiss on his lips.

"Well, thanks to that creature, we no longer have to worry about that."

Ciaryn nods, his eyes turning tender.

"Yes, thanks to him, we have many lifetimes together." His large hand skims over my jaw. "Do you feel different?"

"A bit," I admit. "More whole—more permanent. Though, I've felt that way since I met you. I was alone for many years and now I know I will never be again."

"Never," he vows. "My time as a lone wolf has come to an end as well. We will always be one—this pack will be our safe haven. It will be our home where we start our family. Our children will be raised inside these walls."

Heady thoughts of the future flood me, causing my blood to heat.

"Running a pack, having a mate, becoming a father—are you ready for so much responsibility?"

Ciaryn's grin is filled with tenderness.

"With you by my side, Stella, I can take on anything."

Lowering his head, he captures my lips with his. Our souls knit together as our kiss turns from chaste to hungry. His tongue sweeps into my mouth, tasting me fully. My fingers tunnel into his soft, dark fur and hold tight. Our bodies connect and rub against each other with maddening friction.

Ciaryn's hand slips down my spine before cupping my backside and drawing me flush against his straining cock. His hardness makes my mouth water as I rub my stomach against it. His claws find the lacing of my gown and gently undo it until it falls into a heap at my feet. Kicking off my shoes, I break off our kiss and suck down lungfuls of air.

"Before we get too carried away," I pant. "I'd like to wash up a bit. Cleaning so many wolfmen has left me a bit grimy."

Ciaryn chuckles, slipping my shift off my shoulders and allowing it to join my dress on the ground. Naked and flushed, the firelight licks over my skin. Ciaryn growls as his hand travels up my stomach and gently squeezes my breast. A soft moan slips from my mouth as I tip my body towards his touch. Liquid arousal soaks my inner thighs.

Thumbing my nipple once more, Ciaryn's eyes glow anew.

"Come, I know just the place."

Before I can so much as quirk my brow, Ciaryn scoops me up in his arms. Cradling me to his massive chest, he turns us from our room and out into the corridor. The air in the hall is cool against my heated skin. The only sound is Ciaryn's heavy footsteps as he leads us deeper into the cavern. Darkness swallows us as we travel down corners and crudely carved stairs.

I cling to him, loving the feel of his fur against me. After a few minutes, the air turns humid, and I can hear the faint sound of running water. Taking a sharp right turn, the sight before us steals my breath.

Glowing algae and luminescent plants grow along the pale stone walls and at the bottom of the deep pool. Crystal-clear water flows into the large room and fills the deep underground spring. Steam curls over the lip of the jagged edge of the water.

Carefully, Ciaryn sets me down on the cold floor.

"We should be alone here," Ciaryn purrs in my ear, causing me to shiver. "No one else in the pack ever ventures this deep."

Pleasure washes over me as I take my first step into the pool. Warm water licks up my calf and thigh before stopping just below my shoulders. The gentle lapping of the water soothes my aching muscles. Turning, I watch through half-lidded eyes as Ciaryn undresses with brutal efficiency. His hard cock stands proudly between his thighs, and I suddenly feel very empty.

Biting my lip, I watch him journey around the room with brutal efficiency. He lays out a few clean linen sheets before collecting a bar of soap and a couple of glass jars. Once he settles them along the water's edge, he enters the pool. His dark fur turns slick and molds to his impressive muscles. Taking my hips in his hands, he drags me towards him. He turns me swiftly until my back is settled against him. Ciaryn's cock rests between the cheeks of my ass, seeking entrance into me.

I sigh, twitching against him ever so slightly.

"Naughty," he condemns without heat.

"Always."

His claws click against the stone before I watch him dip a bar of lavender-scented soap into the warm water. Once it foams up to his liking, he drags the bar along my body. He pays special attention to my breasts, teasing my nipples into hardened peaks. Then his hands skim lower, washing between my thighs with efficiency. I lean against him, delighting in the soft caresses that are only heightening my arousal.

Too soon, he is pulling his hand from my intimate flesh and returning to my upper body. Before I can protest, his fingers are digging into the aching muscles of my back. I moan as his strong fingers soothe the soreness. Ciaryn's nose skims up my neck before kissing my cheek.

"You have the softest skin, Stella." His tongue licks over my ear. "It's a struggle not to devour you whole every time I touch you."

"Understandable," I sigh. "I am delicious."

Ciaryn chuckles in my ear before reaching behind him again. He pours a hair tonic from the glass jar onto my head and gently lathers it. His hands rub small circles into my scalp. Pleasure washes over me.

Surprisingly, tears prick my eyes. Never in my life—even as a small child with countless maids and nannies—have I felt so cared for. Each touch is reverent and gentle. My heart aches, not from sadness but from the amount of love pouring from it.

I had spent my early years in fear of my father and my brother. Then, once I was free of them, I flitted from one town to the next, never settling down and making roots. I had always felt lost—as if I was searching for something unknown to me. Now I know what I was looking for. All this time it had been Ciaryn, and every choice I had made brought me to him. To my heart and the other half of my soul. My home is not a place but my wolfman—my mate.

"I love you, Ciaryn," I say in a rush, needing to tell him more than my next breath.

"And I love you. So much." He kisses my cheek before cleansing the suds from my hair.

Turning in his arms, I should offer to bathe him—to show him the same care he's shown me. However, my need to have him inside of me is far more pressing.

Wrapping my arms around his neck, I drag my wet body along his front.

"Now, will you please fuck me, mate? I'm in desperate need of your cock."

Ciaryn's head falls back on a laugh. My cheeks heat but I meant every wanton word.

Cupping me under my ass, Ciaryn walks our soaking bodies out of the warm pool. The air in the room is cool, but his warm body blights any chill. Settling me atop the linen sheet, the stone floor is hard against my back. Any discomfort is soon forgotten as his mouth descends on mine.

He tastes like mint and spice—he tastes like mine. I open my mouth as wide as I can and our tongues meet again, reuniting as if they have been parted for longer than just a few minutes. My thighs slide apart, allowing him closer. Ciaryn's hard cock rests against my stomach and I can feel his seed already leaking from the tip. I moan into his mouth, my hand reaching between us to gently wrap around his length. With the first pump of my hand, Ciaryn's whole body shudders and I swallow his groan.

"You need my cock, don't you? My greedy girl needs to be fucked regularly."

"Yes," I sigh. "Every day."

"Hmm," he hums in his throat. "I don't think once a day will be enough for you. I'll have to knot you repeatedly to assure you of my love."

"Please."

Pulling back, we are both already overwhelmed. His eyes rove over my body taking in my hard nipples to the flush decorating my chest and cheeks. His gaze travels lower to my stomach. It pauses there, snagging on the faint scar left behind from my bullet wound earlier. A low growl echoes around the room. His hand presses over it as if needing the reminder that I'm healed.

"We're both alive, Ciaryn," I remind him. "I am here with you. Forever."

His golden eyes burn into molten amber.

"Forever," he agrees.

Bending down, he kisses the scar, and I shiver. His lips trail hotly across my hips and then down each thigh. He licks over the inside of my knees before focusing on my pussy. My breath rasps out of me as he stares at my pink flesh. I open my legs wider, encouraging him to taste me.

"Beautiful little pussy," he growls. "Look how wet and ready you are. Begging for my tongue and cock."

"Mmm," I agree.

His fur tickles my inner thighs as his mouth lowers to my center. With a quick lick up my slit, I moan into the dimly lit cave. My hands fall to his head, holding him against me as he begins to devour me. In a flurry of teeth, lips, and tongue, my climax is rapidly approaching. Ciaryn licks my clit with the broadside of his tongue as I canter my hips.

One of his hands skims up my thighs before I feel a finger tucking into my entrance. Slowly, he enters me, filling me first with one before adding a second. He curls them expertly until the edges of my vision blur. The sloppy sounds his mouth makes against me are addicting. My muscles begin to tighten in anticipation. A few more twists of his fingers and I'll be done for.

"Come on my face," he commands. "Drown me in your sweetness."

His teeth graze my clit, and I erupt.

White fire licks over my naked skin as my whole body clenches through my climax. My inner walls clamp around his thrusting fingers as he sucks my clit deep into his mouth. Slipping his fingers from me, his tongue spears into my entrance and laps up every ounce of my spend. Once satisfied, he has collected it all—and I am nothing but a twitching mess of nerves—he settles over me.

Sharing my taste with me, his hand falls to my hips. Gently he squeezes me before rolling onto his back and taking me with him. I sit astride him. His rampant cock is trapped between us. I rub myself on it, loving his growl of pleasure.

"Put me inside you," he encourages. "Take your pleasure. Ride me until you come again."

I shiver at his words but do as he says. Wrapping my hands around his hard length, his flesh-colored steel is already slick with my wetness. Lifting up onto my knees, I wiggle around on top until I find my position. Once he is settled, I sink down on him with one punch of my hips. With him buried to the hilt, I moan at the decadent stretch.

Ciaryn's head falls back as his hands drop to my hips. My rhythm is initially disjointed, but I soon find my pace. I rise and fall on his hard cock over and over. My breasts bounce in time with each impale. My mate raises his hips, and he reaches even deeper depths within me. Over and over, I take him as deep as I can.

His hands travel from my hips to my ass and squeeze it gently. He anchors himself with his claws, nearly piercing my flesh, and urges me to move fast. My teeth snap together as I ride him, the pleasure overwhelming. His other hand sneaks between our bodies and finds my clit. Gently, he begins rubbing circles on it and increasing my pleasure.

"You look like a goddess," Ciaryn growls. "I'm fucking a goddess."

The words are said as if in disbelief.

"Ciaryn," I moan. "I'm close."

His hips raise even further, and he grinds his cock into me even harder. His finger on my clit rubs me quicker until my whole body is shaking. My strength is fading, but Ciaryn guides me through it all. My muscles begin to tighten as another climax tears through me. My head falls back as I scream Ciaryn's name.

My mate pounds me through my climax, spurring me on to another one.

"So fucking tight," he snarls. "So perfect."

"Ciaryn," I say, forgetting every word but his name.

Rising quickly, he captures my mouth with a deep kiss before plucking me from his length and settling me on my hands and knees. Looking over my shoulder, I watch him spread the cheeks of my ass and run his tongue along my back entrance with a smirk. His tongue travels lower, spearing into me. I gasp, my arms nearly giving out on top of the linen sheet.

"Ciaryn, please," I beg.

"In a minute, my greedy mate." His teeth bite softly into my ass.

I make a noise of protest, pushing my hips back against him. I need his cock again, and he knows it.

"Now," I demand, my need making my frustration grow.

His tongue glides up my spine, tasting my sweat and the water dripping from my wet hair. Once his lips are on my shoulder, he presses a kiss to my claiming mark, tasting it lovingly.

Then, after what feels like an eternity, I feel the head of his cock pushing into me.

"Yes," I moan. "Fuck me."

Ciaryn nips my shoulder, not hard enough to break the skin but enough to set my blood on fire.

"I'll do more than just fuck you," he growls. "My knot needs to be buried in your little cunt once more."

My mouth opens with a moan. A delicious shiver goes through me. Ciaryn retreats only to plunge deep. His hips smack up against my ass, and I feel the ridge of his knot against my opening. Again, he retreats and plunges deep. My fingers curl into the linens as I try to keep myself upright.

Ciaryn wraps the long length of my hair around his fist and snatches it back. My head falls back as he powers into me over and over again. His cock butts up against my womb as he takes me over and over again. With each thrust, I feel his knot harden. I begin clenching down on his cock, another climax looming when I finally feel him breach me with it.

The pain is immediate, but it is also fleeting. Once he is deep inside me, I feel his knot swell and seal the two of us together. After a moment, my body is quickening again, and pleasure rolls through me. Wave after wave of climax washes over me, and I clench down on his pulsing cock.

Ciaryn's hand drops my hair and takes hold of my hips tightly. Rolling himself, he rocks back and forth inside me, moving as much as he can with the knot tying us together. My fingers claw at the stone floor as another climax rocks through me.

"Come inside me, mate," I say, locking eyes with him over my shoulder. "Fill me with your seed. Get me pregnant."

The words are out before I can take them back. I had ideas of wanting to wait to start a family, but now I'm unsure if I do. Perhaps I won't take the contraceptive herbs and instead will let nature take its course. I can't think of anything more perfect than us having a child. The final piece in solidifying our family.

Ciaryn's whole body tenses at my command. His claws prick the skin of my hips as he hauls himself harder against me. I come with another cry and Ciaryn follows me. My name is a harsh growl on his tongue. His seed bathes my inner walls, flooding me with torrent after torrent of hot spend. Without the knot, it'd leak out of me in a steady stream.

Instead, it's all locked inside me, solidifying our bond and tethering our souls together.

Once his cock twitches but releases no more come, he falls panting against my back. Our hearts echo each other, pounding with intensity. His mouth leaves lazy kisses against my spine. My legs and arms tremble as little licks of pleasure still assault me.

Wrapping his strong forearms beneath me, Ciaryn lifts me still impaled on his length. We'll be joined together like this for some time. My eyes threaten to shut as I feel him carry us back down the dark hall. We return to our room in no time, and he settles me atop the silks and overstuffed pillows.

I sigh deeply as he drapes a heavy arm across my waist. His lips press kisses to my cheek and temple. Sleepily I turn towards him, all my energy waning, but I have enough for one final declaration. After death loomed so close today, I couldn't feel more alive and at peace.

"I love you," I whisper.

"I love you," he returns.

Our bond becomes tangible with our declarations and wraps us in a fine thread of gold. Whether it is real or just my exhaustion making me see things, I hardly care. Ciaryn is mine, and I am his.

Forever.

A revenant has come to collect the bodies that litter at our den's opening.

I remember the first time I saw such a creature: drinking the blood of a dying man as if it had been a starving animal. That description doesn't seem too inaccurate, given its skeletal frame hidden beneath its tattered black cloak and clanking metal armor.

He must be desperate to wander this far. The corpses are those of the hunters who came for my mate a year ago. Due to being exposed to the elements, their mortal forms are little more than sun-bleached bones and ripped cloth. Still, that matters little to a revenant. I have seen them dine on bones until there is no trace of a body having been there.

Blood they prefer, but a creature of their ilk will take any part of a body they can find. I suppress my shudder as I watch it through narrowed eyes. Lukar is at my side, ready to strike if it ventures too close. Ever since he found his mate, Wren, a few moons ago, he's been even more protective of our home. Not that I can blame him.

The revenant's bony hand reaches for one of the hunter's

rib bones. He breaks it with a simple snap and brings it towards its face. Nodding towards Lukar, I prowl through the cavern's opening.

"Leave," I command. "You are not welcome here."

The revenant barely lifts its head. Its frayed cloak blows on a gentle breeze carrying the scent of decay.

"No one welcomes death, yet I arrive. You would do well to remember that, wolf."

Its voice is a broken whisper—the last rasping words of a deadman.

"Are you threatening me?"

The creature merely waves a frail hand.

"I'm too hungry for ideal threats. Bored, too."

I raise up on my haunches, and my ears flatten to my head.

"Sounds like you could use a companion."

Again, the creature laughs weakly.

"My kind is solitary."

I have no idea why I wish to press this issue. I should be running this foul creature off, but I find myself curious instead. It may be because I understand this revenant to some degree. If I had not found Stella, I would be in a similar position. Alone, unhappy, a ghost of the wolf I was meant to be.

"Are there no females of your kind?" I ask, genuinely curious.

The revenant levels a stare at me. Its eyes are hollow. The faint glow inside them barely flickering.

"No."

"Then how has your kind come to be? Do you mate with human females as we do?"

The look in its dead eyes causes a chill to break out across the clearing. I back up a step, and my muscles tense anticipating an attack should the creature make one. After a heavy beat of silence, the revenant's mouth twists.

"What kind of female would allow a death omen into her bed?"

I open my mouth, but the creature merely snatches up a pale arm bone and disappears into a whisper of dark fabric. I stare after him. His unanswered question lingers in the empty clearing. Indeed, what kind of female would want to lie with such a creature? Though I'm sure the same could be asked of the human women who have mated my kind.

If the revenant seeks companionship, I have no doubt he'll find it someday. However, until then, I don't want him or any more of his kind coming too close to our home.

"I'll send more to join you for patrols," I say to Lukar, who has come to stand by my side. "Until we are sure no more of his kind are coming."

Lukar bows his head before taking off towards *The Woods*. I watch him disappear into the thicket before I prowl back through the den's opening. The once-quiet cavern hums with life. Wolfmen and humans alike bustle about in a steady stream of everyday chores and duties.

A soft laugh echoes from a few feet away, and my blood heats instantly. As if her sweet scent wasn't already luring me towards her, the sound of her voice certainly is.

Near the center of the den, I find her dressed in the simple green gown I saw her dress in this morning. She is talking with Brydon and his mate Elaine—a human woman of thirty, with whom Brydon crossed paths on his way back from town. Her horse had fallen and trapped her beneath it. Brydon had brought her back here, where Stella mended her broken leg, and she and him fell deeply in love as he saw to her recovery.

Love. There has been so much of it since that creature appeared and saved my Stella. Whatever mating blight my pack had been under was done away with overnight. Stella and I may have been the first pairing, but we are far from the last. Our pack's legacy will continue for generations.

Especially our line as I watch my mate rest a hand on her swollen stomach.

She is only a few months along and already showing a considerable amount. Pride floods my chest as I take her in. Stella is the most beautiful female I've ever seen, but somehow, during the year we have been together, her beauty has grown. Now, as she is round with our child, her loveliness nearly sends me to my knees.

I approach her slowly, coming to her side and wrapping my arm around her waist. Her smile is brilliant as she stares up at me. I kiss her softly, delighting in her taste.

"Alpha," both Brydon and Elaine say. I nod politely at them and tuck Stella firmly into my side.

"Thank you for the pain-relieving herbs, Stella. My leg always hurts before it's about to rain."

"Happy to help," my mate says before bidding the other two goodbye.

She turns into my embrace. Reaching between us, I run my hand down her stomach before lifting it in my hands. Stella lets out a soft moan, and her eyes glaze over.

"That feels wonderful." Her hand rests atop mine. "I missed you."

We have barely been apart for two hours, yet it feels like years since I last had her in my arms.

"I missed you, mate. How are you feeling? Are your back and feet still aching?"

She wrinkles her adorable nose and I suppress the urge to kiss it.

"A bit. Why did no one warn me how much your feet swell during pregnancy? I'm tempted to go barefoot until the babe is born."

She lifts her mouth towards mine indicating she wants a kiss. I happily oblige her as our mouths move over each other.

"Besides that, I'm fine, Ciaryn. You need not fuss over me so much."

I shake my head.

"When I found out you were pregnant, I should've demanded you remain in our bed where I could keep watch over you."

We talked about waiting—about going on adventures and traveling. However, both of us had already seen all of the world we wanted to see. Together, we decided that our next adventure would be starting our family and making our lives even fuller.

"But, as I said before, I hate being idle and while my feet may hurt I'd much rather be on them than spending my days doing nothing," she reminds me.

"Stubborn mate," I sigh.

"But you love me regardless?"

"Of course I do."

Stella grins and her blue eyes sparkle up at me.

"I have many months of pregnancy ahead of me Ciaryn. Once I get too big, I'm sure I'll be longing for the days I can lie in bed from sun up to sun down. Until then, I have responsibilities as mistress of this pack."

"Indeed, with so many new human females here, there's never a shortage of things to be done," I agree.

As head healer, Stella has been busy training other women in her skills. Every day I am more in awe of her than the last. Truly I am the most fortunate male to call her mine.

"But," Stella says, her grin turning wicked. "I've finished most of my tasks for the day and could be persuaded to get off my feet for a few hours if you wanted to keep me company."

She bats her golden eyelashes at me and my cock hardens in an instant.

My desire flames to life as I take in her blatant invitation. Without warning, I scoop her into my arms, and her riot of giggles makes my heart swell. She clings to me as she has always done—the same way she held me from that first evening when I took her from her home and into my life forever.

Making the journey to our room quickly, I set her down for only a moment. I slip her loose gown over her head and toss it away. Her shift follows next, leaving her clad in only her simple wool stockings. In addition to her round stomach, her breasts have also grown with her pregnancy.

I gently thumb one of her nipples, and she whimpers. Stella has always been responsive, but now all of her senses are heightened. There are days when a few kisses to her neck and a brush of my claws against her clit make her scream her release. I am the most fortunate of males.

Lifting her into my arms, I settle her into the silk atop our pallet. Our scents have become one, and our joint smell lingers everywhere in the room. I inhale her honey scent greedily as I kiss down her body. She thrusts her hips towards me. Her pink flesh is already dripping wet, begging for my tongue and cock even though she had both inside of her only a few hours ago.

"Please, Ciaryn," Stella whimpers. "I ache for you."

Oh, that will not do.

Giving my mate what she needs, I kiss her clit before spearing my tongue into her. Curling it a few times, I reach far into her inner depths and feel her delicate muscles clamp around me. Her hands hold my head as she grinds her climax out on my face. I taste her sweetness, lapping it all up before tucking a finger into her tight channel.

Once she is panting again, I replace my finger with my cock. The ridge of my knot is already formed. A flush erupts over Stella's chest and cheeks, turning her deliciously pink. I meet her mouth with my own and swallow each of her throaty moans. Her little cunt grips me so tightly my head spins.

Her wetness coats my thrusting cock, aiding me to go even deeper inside her.

"Ciaryn!" she cries, clawing at my back.

I know what she wants without having to tell me. My claws tickle her clit, and her whole body tightens as she cries. At the crest of her climax, I breech her with my knot, sealing her to me. Our souls and hearts become one. By tethering us together, I can taste our love and feel it wrapping around us.

Her sharp inhale makes me kiss her harder until all she feels is pleasure. She comes again, her eyes open but unseeing. My name is slurred from her lips as her body goes limp. The sight of her spread out before me ignites my blood. I take in her swollen mouth and the savage bite on her shoulder, marking her as mine. I take in her full breasts and round stomach, and I let the pleasure kindle inside of me.

My spine tingles before snapping straight and pushing deep inside her. With a growl, I feel my come fill her in a rush. Torrent after torrent stays locked between the two of us. Once the last of my seed is spent, I roll us onto our sides so that I can cradle her stomach. The sound of pleasure she makes sends a shiver down my spine.

I stare at my mate—her flushed, freckled cheeks and golden hair. Her eyes are tired but full of enough love to steal my breath. We were both alone for so long. Even when I had my father, it was only when he was a shell of a male he had once been. Not until I found Stella did I feel like I belonged somewhere. My place has always been by her side, wherever that may be.

A yawn sneaks up on her. The pregnancy has made her tired lately. The golden light streaming in from the corridor makes her glow. She looks every bit the goddess I always tell her she is.

"Perfect," I murmur, tucking a piece of hair behind her ear. "Beautiful."

Pink dots her cheeks, and it's a wonder she can still blush after all we've done and said to each other. Our legs tangle together, and I cradle her close.

"When I was a girl, I never even imagined I could feel like this. Happy, safe, and well-cared for." Her eyes fill with unshed tears. "I have you to thank for that."

Whoever she was before this and whatever horrors she lived through are far from this place. No one will take her from me. I have spilled blood for her before and will gladly do so again should the need arise. I kiss her brow, silently vowing all of this to her.

"Whatever the future holds, we will face it together."

Stella smiles. The love in her eyes steals my breath and makes me hold her closer.

"Always."

DON'T MISS THE NEXT ONE!

A death omen and the human woman who makes him feel alive! Coming October 2025.

READ MY OTHER BOOKS!

Interconnected monster romance standalone on Kindle Unlimited!

Short and spicy monster romance novellas following a different diabolical looking creature!

Holiday-themed monster romances for those who want a little extra spice on Kindle Unlimited!

ACKNOWLEDGMENTS

I want to thank all of you for picking up *A Kiss From a Wolfman*! This was my first time writing knotting and I hope you all enjoyed! Ciaryn is definitely one of my most monstrous looking men.

I'd like to thank my beta/ARC teams, my patrons, and all of you who've shared or continue to support my work. You all are my own personal love potion!

See you in the next one!

xoxo Charlotte

ABOUT THE AUTHOR

Charlotte Swan is twenty-six year old, living in Chicago. When she is not dreaming about being whisked away to a world filled with magic and sexy monsters, she is busy being a freelance social media marketer and full-time smut lover. To read her debut novel *Taken by the Dark Elf King*, hear about her upcoming projects, or to connect with her on social media please find her on her website or by scanning the code below.

www.authorcharlotteswan.com